When a Girl is Born

It is China at the turn of th
glad when a girl is born.
property, a burden on the
married off as soon as possible.

Ko-chin is fourteen years old. She has been taught never
to ask questions, and knows that she must always accept
whatever happens to her. But all that changes when she
is married off to her new husband—a reformer who tells
her she must think for herself and be a new woman in
a modern world. He says that together they can change
things for themselves and for China. But can they? And
when China finds itself in the middle of rebellion, and
people are being murdered in the streets, how can Ko-
chin choose between her old traditions and the new
western ways?

Pamela Grant has always been interested in China, and for her
Doctorate she specialized in the connections between the past and
present in Chinese history. *When a Girl is Born* was her first novel.
Her hobbies include gardening, drama, and local history.

WHEN A GIRL IS BORN

Pamela Grant

OXFORD
UNIVERSITY PRESS

OXFORD
UNIVERSITY PRESS

Great Clarendon Street, Oxford OX2 6DP

Oxford University Press is a department of the University of Oxford.
It furthers the University's objective of excellence in research, scholarship,
and education by publishing worldwide in

Oxford New York

Auckland Cape Town Dar es Salaam Hong Kong Karachi
Kuala Lumpur Madrid Melbourne Mexico City Nairobi
New Delhi Shanghai Taipei Toronto

With offices in

Argentina Austria Brazil Chile Czech Republic France Greece
Guatemala Hungary Italy Japan Poland Portugal Singapore
South Korea Switzerland Thailand Turkey Ukraine Vietnam

Oxford is a registered trade mark of Oxford University Press
in the UK and in certain other countries

First published 1993
First published in this paperback edition 2001

British Library Cataloguing in Publication Data available

ISBN-13: 978-0-19-275186-7

Paper used in the production of this book is a natural, recyclable product
made from wood grown in the sustainable forests.
The manufacturing process conforms to the environmental regulations of the
country or origin.

For my mother,
the girl born Ruth Thacker,
with my love

CONTENTS

Note on Pronunciation

Chinese and Western pronunciation are very different from one another. As a rough guide, Ko-chin's name would be pronounced 'Gore-jin'; Mo-ch'o as 'More-chore'; the 'ao' of Han Lao is pronounced 'ow' as in 'how'; and Lan-kuei sounds like 'Lan-gway'.

In the Forbidden City . . .

           . . . the Pearl Concubine slowly raised her shining head. She had begun to think the sun would never set today, the drumbeats roll through the cramped alleys to warn every whole man, save one, that it was time to leave or die. Her breathing quickened. Would that one man dare to summon her to his bedchamber tonight? Because see him she must.

Already the vast Throne Room's golden ceilings and tall red columns would be deep in shadow, state officials in their sedans urging on the bent-backed coolies who carried them over the white marble pavements to the great gates. Soon this city within a city would be left to those part-men, the eunuchs, and the women whose sole concern was the service of the Emperor of the Celestial Empire, China. Four thousand of them lived here in this enclave beneath the darkening sky: the Pearl Concubine was the only one of them the Emperor trusted.

The Emperor, Son of Heaven: the pale oval face of the girl was very still, her onyx eyes beneath moth eyebrows blank, as she remembered how eight years ago he had chosen her for his Empress from the fourteen-year-old Manchu virgins paraded for his choice. But had he ever really believed that his tigerish aunt would let a girl who shared his passionate interest in that strange new world to the West be so close to him? But at least she had been allowed to become his concubine—and his co-conspirator! Because, as yet, neither his aunt nor the creature she had made Empress had discovered their secret.

The Pearl's eyes sparkled as they slid towards the table, where she had set the latest parcel of books and letters smuggled into the Forbidden City. The shock of finding them gone took her breath away for a moment. Then she called her serving woman.

The woman's eyes slithered away at the accusation. 'I have touched nothing, lady,' she whined.

The Pearl smiled coldly. 'Do not think me so powerless that I could not arrange for you to disappear as easily as any unwanted baby girl,' she said softly. 'First give me what is mine, then help me prepare for the Emperor's bed.'

'*If* he sends for you, lady . . . '

'He will send, and if you flout me, he shall be told,' the Pearl returned evenly and, suddenly white-faced, the woman ran to obey. The torturers of the Forbidden City were renowned.

The fastenings of the parcel had not been touched but the Pearl dared not show relief: in this place, where the façade of power itself had cracked, gone rotten, every life hung by a thread. Had it not been for the great plan she shared with the Emperor, she would have swallowed opium long ago. So now, with a steady hand, she massaged into her face the white mutton fat the servant warmed between her hands, then masked the cleansed and softened skin with powder of fine-ground rice and lead. When she had drawn in her fine eyebrows with the brush dipped in oiled ink, she snapped, 'My rouge, woman.'

The servant, hands unsteady enough for both of them, pressed a silken pad steeped in rose-petal paste to each white cheek, then watched the Pearl dab with red the centre of her lower lip. Ah, this girl might be beautiful, but one day soon she would be snuffed out!

The summons to the Emperor's bedchamber came at moonrise. Tall and slender in her gown of rose and gold, her coiled and jewelled hair fragrant with oil of cassia, the Pearl slipped off her shoes. Their six-inch stacked heels would have made a fox fairy heavy-footed, and long ago the Emperor's aunt had made sure the only way from the Empress's and concubines' apartments to those of the Emperor passed over her own verandah—which creaked.

Tonight of all nights, Tz'u-hsi must not know who passed, discover what the Emperor's favourite carried with her. Heart hammering, the Pearl edged over the polished boards where only the monsters' heads bristling from the curved roof above her head could see her pass; and the silence, that held in chill splendour the soaring eaves and golden roofs, remained unbroken.

In the Imperial bedchamber, sullen eunuchs had put aside the Emperor's yellow dragon robes, slipped his red silk bedshirt over his head and retired. Alone on his huge bronze bed amid yellow satin coverings, he scowled at the five-clawed dragons that coiled on every carven surface. If only he himself had a dragon's heart . . . but this Emperor knew that he had been broken long ago. All he had left was his Pearl. As the curtain twitched aside, he opened his arms wide.

Outside the bedchamber, in every Imperial apartment, the clocks and watches, that it was three eunuchs' full-time duty to keep wound, ticked away the last year before a storm to shake the Forbidden City to its foundations broke. Beyond its walls, the same moonlight shone down on the houses of the foreign ambassadors his aunt so hated: in their barbarian calendar, it was the year of 1897.

CHAPTER 1
GOLDEN LILIES

On the next day, in a little town far from the gilded Forbidden City, Ko–chin and Mo–ch'o found their stern, dignified mother, who never wept, in tears.

'What is it, our mother?' cried Ko–chin, terrified.

Shadowed eyes, drowned in bitterness, stared back at her. 'You will find out soon enough, daughter.' She swayed across the room on her tiny feet but at the door-curtain paused, muttering more to herself than to them, ' "How sad it is to be framed in woman's form! Nothing on earth is held so cheap!" ' Then, 'Get on with your work, girls,' and she left them alone.

Ko–chin did not move. Timidly Mo–ch'o touched her arm, whispering, 'Sister . . . ?' but Ko–chin was deep in thought. When had she heard those words, 'How sad it is . . . ', from an ancient poem, before? Yes! On the day that Eldest Sister had been wrenched screaming from Mother's arms! 'So much fuss,' Father had shouted, 'the creature will be fed and clothed there. What more does she expect?'

'As your daughter, more than to be sent as plaything for the men of the Yang household to pay your debts!' Mother had flung back at him.

She had been beaten for that, while Ko–chin and Mo–ch'o stood by helplessly, sick with new knowledge. So that was what growing up could mean. They had never heard of Eldest Sister again, but since then the family's fortunes had improved—in fact, so much so that Brother Huang thought himself quite a gentleman these days, thought Ko–chin with a curl of her lip.

Small, hot hands tugged at her. 'Come back, sister,' Mo–ch'o was sobbing. 'Your soul wanders from your body!'

'Silly child. I was only—dreaming,' Ko-chin told her shakily. 'There's nothing for you to cry about.'

But Mo-ch'o choked, 'There is! Because I know why Mother was crying like that—they've found you a husband.'

Ko-chin's heart stood still. Of course. The boy to whom she had been betrothed at birth had died a year ago, but Father would have been looking for a new bridegroom now that she was fourteen years old. She licked dry lips and muttered, 'If that's true, little sister, why cry? At least you and I will have husbands and honourable positions, not like poor Eldest Sister.'

'You will,' choked Mo-ch'o, 'but how long will the husband to whom I am given love an ugly woman?'

Fiercely, Ko-chin caught her sister's slight body into her arms. Mo-ch'o was tiny for her twelve years. Underfed as a baby, now her skin was blotchy, her teeth brown, her hair thin and lank. 'Such rubbish,' Ko-chin breathed against her cheek. 'Think of your tiny feet! Not a fraction more than three inches, when my great things are at least four inches long!'

Mo-ch'o managed a wintry smile. 'That's because when Mother binds them even tighter I don't undo the bandages the way you did. But, oh, sister, how can Mother bear to hurt us like that?'

Ko-chin rocked her gently. 'Because she knows that no girl with big feet like a peasant's can make a good marriage, of course. So, dry your eyes and think how pleased your husband will be with your tiny feet.'

Mo-ch'o dabbed her face with her sleeve, sniffing, 'I—I suppose the old Man in the Moon has already tied my leg to my husband's with invisible red silk, hasn't he?'

'Of course he has,' Ko-chin told her. And her own as well . . . who would he be?

That night, her mother told her. Ko-chin stared in stunned disbelief. 'You cannot mean old Merchant Chen! Not that dreadful old man who the servants say—'

'He it is, child,' broke in her mother tonelessly. 'It is my fate to send a second daughter unprotected into the world, to serve my husband's business interests.' And with a dry sob she stumbled from the room on her bound feet.

That night Ko-chin made no prayers to Kuan-yin, Goddess of Mercy. Instead, stretched rigid on her bed, other lines from that hateful poem ran through her brain again and again:

'A boy that comes to a home
Drops to earth like a god that chooses to be born.
No one is glad when a girl is born;
By her the family sets no store . . . '

How true it was, she thought bitterly. Brother Huang is like a god in this household and we girls count for nothing—not even with Mother, really; she's always going to the temple to pray for more sons. But it's not her fault—she knows daughters will be of no use to her when she's old. By then we'll belong to our husbands' families and be looking after their mothers! Bringing up a girl was a duty every family was glad to be rid of—and now it was her turn to go.

Ko-chin was listlessly dusting the carved blackwood chairs the next morning with an oiled feather when Huang seized her arm and propelled her out into the courtyard where his friends sat drinking tea around the goldfish pool.

'Walk,' hissed Huang with a push. Then he announced loudly, 'Do not say again that girls' feet should not be bound, Han-lao, until you have seen how charmingly my sister sways along on her golden lilies!'

Only one young man did not turn his shocked face away but, although that one held her eyes with his, there was no boldness in his look and the staggering thought seared Ko-chin's numbed mind: 'He's sorry for me!' Then Huang's hand was shoving her back into the house. There, turning to flash one look of scalding contempt at her brother, she heard an angry young voice declare, 'By shaming your sister, Huang, you shame yourself. Come, friends, it is time we left.'

Shamed, and deliberately, by her own brother: for Huang knew as well as she did that no decent girl was ever seen by men from outside her own family. He might as well have publicly declared her a flower girl, a common prostitute—'Which is all I shall be in the Chen family,' she told herself fiercely, 'after old Merchant Chen has tired of me.' But the memory of the way that tall young man had looked at her mercifully blotted out that thought for the moment. Was he the 'Han-lao', who had angered her brother by saying footbinding should be forbidden? Why, she thought wonderingly, he had looked at her as if he saw even a woman as another human being, rather than a mere thing to be used. Perhaps being married wouldn't seem so bad if she could be sent to a bridegroom like that . . .

The very next day the message came. The cook's wife slipped it from her wide sleeve into Ko-chin's hand as they passed in the courtyard. Heart pounding, Ko-chin retreated to a quiet corner and unfolded the paper. Black characters with firm strong brush-strokes declared, 'Courage: you shall not go to old Chen. My word on it.' Then she read the signature aloud: 'Li Han-lao.'

So that look had meant something—perhaps everything. Feverishly, she screwed the paper up. If anyone discovered it . . . Not until it had gone up in flames on the cooking fire did she begin to think. How had Han-lao known she could read? Most girls were never taught—it brought down their marriage value. And of which Li family in the town was he a son? 'I know I can never see him again,' she muttered to herself, 'and that he can do no more to save me than Mother but, oh, it helps to know someone cares!'

But for all that, as soon as a chance came, she drew aside the cook's wife and whispered, 'Who gave you that message?'

'The gardener's wife from that grand Li house on the hill,' the woman whispered back, 'and she was given good silver for her trouble!'

Ko-chin only hesitated for a moment. Better her mother should ask where her one gold bracelet was than that this woman should ever breathe a word about the message.

'My lips are sealed about the young master,' hissed the woman as her hands closed greedily on the bracelet.

'So are mine,' Ko-chin thought, 'but I can think about him!'

That night she stared for a long time into the patchy mirror she and Mo-ch'o shared. The face that looked back at her was certainly not beautiful enough for Han-lao to have fallen in love with her at a glance. Ko-chin sighed; that kind of thing only happened in fairy tales, not to an ordinary girl like her. And, anyway, he must be at least eighteen or nineteen years old and long since wed to the girl his parents had chosen for him.

Ko-chin's sigh this time was loud enough to wake Mo-ch'o. The little girl scrambled out of bed, whimpering as her bound feet touched the floor, and clapped a dismayed hand to her mouth as Ko-chin exclaimed furiously, 'Golden lilies indeed! It is poets who should be drowned at birth, not baby girls! The man who coined that pretty phrase for bound feet should try binding his own—feel the pain, smell the stink when he changes the bindings! I wonder if his mother's feet mortified and dropped off because they had been bound too tightly? Oh, but, sister, there are young men who—'

She stopped abruptly and Mo-ch'o, eyes wide with amazement, repeated, 'Young men? But, Ko-chin, how can you know—?'

8

'I was being foolish,' broke in Ko-chin hastily. 'Back into bed, sister, and make room for me.'

As the days passed with no further word, and the horoscopes cast for herself and her bridegroom were found favourable, the last fugitive hope that Han-lao could really save her died in Ko-chin's heart. Even her mother had withdrawn completely from her: it was no use turning for comfort there. 'I thought she cared at least a little for me,' Ko-chin complained to Mo-ch'o one long afternoon, 'but she doesn't even look at me now, let alone speak.'

Mo-ch'o didn't answer. Small head cocked, she wasn't even listening, thought Ko-chin irritably. 'I might as well be gone from this house already,' she began, but Mo-ch'o hissed, 'Ssh! Someone has come—I think it is our mother's brother. Come to bid you farewell, maybe? Here's Cook's fat wife come to fetch you!'

Ko-chin swiftly smoothed her hair and, hurrying to her mother's rooms, tried to smooth her thoughts, too. However badly she felt herself to be treated, she had been too well trained ever to show those feelings. So, with blank face and lowered eyes she entered the room to bow before her uncle.

'So you are to be married, my niece,' he murmured, 'and it is farewell between us. Your wedding gifts will, of course, be surrendered to your husband's family but I have brought you this one thing for yourself.'

Shyly Ko-chin raised her eyes to his long fine hands and what they held. 'For me?' she breathed. 'Oh, Uncle!' Then the little Kuan-yin of white jade lay in her hands, cool and serene. Her own Goddess of Mercy. How like this kindly man, who had taught first her mother, then herself and Mo-ch'o to read, to understand how badly she needed comfort.

'It pleases you, my niece?' her uncle was asking. 'Then remember, when you have sons, that just as a piece of rough jade has to be cut, ground, carved, polished, so a man must be taught to become restrained, courteous, learned and refined.'

'I will remember, honourable uncle,' whispered Ko-chin. 'How can I thank you?' Though, in the cold shadow of her future, could even Kuan-yin come to her aid?

'Daughter—'

Ko-chin looked up, startled. Why was Mother looking so strangely at her? Had she found out about the missing bracelet or—far worse—how it came to be lost? She clenched her hands around the Kuan-yin, trying to still their shaking, as she cried, 'Have I offended you, my mother, or—or is there worse news for me? Am I now to be only a concubine, not a wife . . . ?'

Her mother's pale lips twitched. 'Always so dramatic. Child, have I not taught you better than to make such a display of yourself, and before your uncle, too!'

But Ko-chin's whole being was concentrated into one burning question: what had changed? When she knew that, she would remember her manners again.

Her mother drew a long breath. 'Daughter, you are no longer to marry Mr Chen. Your father's debt to that gentleman has been settled and the way to a most advantageous business arrangement opened to him—in exchange for you.'

Han-lao had saved her after all! Oh, far better his concubine than wife to any other—tears rolled down Ko-chin's flushed cheeks and her mother looked at her sharply. 'Do not rejoice yet, child,' she snapped. 'I fear you are too much honoured and all may yet come to grief for you, as bride to the fourth son of a family so far above our station.'

This was beyond believing. Into the sudden silence, her uncle said quietly, 'The times are changing. The reign of the August Personage of Jade in Heaven draws, I think, to a close.'

Ko-chin forgot herself enough then to look directly into her uncle's eyes and cry, 'I pray you to explain, honoured uncle! For how can any change in Heaven affect the fate of so lowly a being as myself?'

The old man shook his head. 'Such impatience! You would have had a short life in the courts of Chen, my child. Well, it seems that Mr Li's fourth son saw you—through no fault of your mother's,' he added hastily, glimpsing the expression on his sister's face, 'and, as he is just as impatient as you are, he decided then and there that he would have you for his bride. But it is a sad error for a father so to indulge a son's whims, whatever honour that son may have won for his family by passing high in the Imperial State Examinations.'

He tutted to himself for a moment, then went on, 'Of course, the boy should have been safely married long ago, but the girl died just before the wedding. Even so . . . '

Ko-chin tried to swallow. It was true: she was to marry Han-lao. She felt her uncle's disapproving eyes on her as he murmured, 'It seems that more than one did some looking that day. No modesty! But you will reap the harvest, niece, for there will be no quiet life for you within the courts of the Li family.'

'You mean his mother?' Ko-chin faltered. 'She will hate me, surely, so poor a match for her son—'

'Of that you need have no doubt,' confirmed her mother grimly. 'But that is not what my brother meant. You will not be living in her courts.'

'Not—' But where else would she live, waiting for her sons to be born, humbly obedient to mother-in-law and to husband's brothers' wives? Ko-chin shook her head dazedly, whispering, 'I do not understand.'

'Who can understand so wayward a son?' returned her uncle sternly. 'Alas, Li Han-lao intends to take you with him when he returns to his government position in Peking.'

After Ko-chin's unbelieving gasp, there was silence. Sunshine filtered through the rice paper that latticed the carved window frames; its pearly light fell softly on the worn grey tiles of the floor and gave a sombre radiance to the dark furnishings. Dust motes danced in the moving air, but still no one spoke. What was there to say? This young man was shaking the customs of long centuries to their roots.

'But will his mother allow that I go?' Ko-chin stammered at last.

The old man laid his hand on her smooth head. 'She has no choice. Since there are already grandsons in plenty, his father has consented. Doubtless when you bear a son, Li Han-lao will send you to his parents' home again for the child to be properly reared. Yet, who knows, my little Ko-chin? There is a great storm brewing and in Peking, I fear, you will be in its very midst. Now, where is my stick?' Ko-chin handed him his silver-topped cane and he rose stiffly to his feet. 'We shall not meet again, my niece, for should you ever return I shall by then have passed to the Land of Extreme Felicity in the West. And so, farewell. May Kuan-yin protect you.'

Ko-chin's mother sighed as the door-curtain closed behind him: 'Alas, my daughter, I am almost as afraid for you as I was before. What kind of young man can this Li Han-lao be, to care so little for the happiness of his family and his duty to his ancestors?'

But Ko-chin could not be daunted now. She slipped a hand inside her mother's, whispering, 'Honourable uncle is never wrong, my mother—the times are changing. They must be, for this to happen at all, and one day soon daughters may no longer have to swallow bitterness!'

'Ai-ya, how young and foolish you still are, daughter,' was all her mother said to that, adding grudgingly, 'But, if you bear many sons, it may be that in time the Li family will forgive you.'

'Sons?' echoed Ko-chin, eyes suddenly radiant. And she had been wondering however she could repay him for his kindness! Oh, she would give him such sons that his family would rejoice at the day he set eyes on her!

CHAPTER 2

THE RED SEDAN

Ko-chin, awake before dawn on her wedding day, traced with a cold finger her tingling hairline: that aunt had enjoyed jerking out the stray hairs from her forehead and temples yesterday, before putting up her hair to show she was now a grown woman! It would be no hardship if she never saw *her* again. But to leave Mother, little Mo-ch'o—Ko-chin's eyes filled with tears as she knelt before her little Kuan-yin, praying for courage. Then she went to her mother to take the bitter medicine that would stop her bladder filling as fast as usual, so that the day's long hours of sitting would be a little less unendurable. She could not help squeaking, though, at the relentless cleansing that followed.

'Be silent, girl,' snapped her mother. 'Do you want it said that a bride from this house took sickness into her new home? Now, Mo-ch'o, fetch me her gown.'

The last hours in the only home she had known raced by but Ko-chin's mute misery only broke in the last moments, when she saw her father's face: 'Oh, he smiles wide enough now he sees me in red bridal clothes!' she hissed to Mo-ch'o. 'Red means joy for him, but what joy would there be for me if I was going to the husband he chose?'

Strange, this new emotion welling up inside her, bursting out into resentful words. Girls were not supposed to feel anger, let alone express it, but for a moment it helped when she heard her mother cry above Mo-ch'o's sobs, 'May the red sedan bear you to a happier fate than my own, daughter!' Then she was bundled out of the door and into the suffocating blackness of a curtained sedan.

Eyes strained wide against the darkness, Ko-chin crammed her fingers into her mouth against the scream struggling to escape as the sedan rocked into motion. Now she was on her own as never before—could the noise of firecrackers sputtering outside really drive off the hungry spirits that flocked around a bridal sedan? Even though they knew the terrified girl shut inside had, for the space of her journey between one home and another, no place in the world of living human beings? Neither child nor woman, she was such easy prey—but everyone said noise frightened them away . . . What good was that, though, if she suffocated before she reached her journey's end? Desperately Ko-chin gulped at the stifling air of her tiny jolting prison. She must not fail her bridegroom; he had saved the child Ko-chin, but that child had died when she had passed out of her father's house. It was the woman Ko-chin, reborn as his wife once she had passed the threshold into his family's home, who would repay his kindness.

Ko-chin slithered into unconsciousness even as the curtains of her prison were twitched aside, but seconds later her eyes flew open again as the flood of light poured in, reviving even as it dazzled her. Tears flooded down her face as, seized by strangers' hands, she was further dazzled by the flashing of mirrors from every direction—whatever they thought of her, the Li family did not intend the spirits, as afraid of light as sound, to seize this new bride on her brief passage between sedan and enclosing walls.

'It's over—my old life—over forever—oh, Mother!' Broken phrases raced through Ko-chin's mind as, safely within doors again, she obediently bowed and knelt to the strangers all around her, repeated the words that made her wife to the tall figure at her side. It would have been a comfort to glimpse his face—it had been a kind face, hadn't it?—but Ko-chin did not dare glance upward. She could already feel, like cold water, the hatred of the women clustering round, hear them muttering about the disgraceful circumstances of her betrothal. Bad enough to have seen him once, in their eyes . . .

Then he was gone and she was given over to those women to be taught, as new brides were always taught, just how low her place in this household was. Body rigid, the delicate lines of her face set and dark eyes glazed, Ko-chin looked no longer living girl but perfect sculpture. This was what she had expected. It would have been worse in the household of old Chen, because then it would not have been Han-lao waiting for her in the bedchamber later . . . Ko-chin shuddered and harsh laughter punctuated the volley of insults hurled at her. Only once did she flinch, though, when a girl little older than herself jeered, 'Such an unnatural creature will never bear sons!' Otherwise, she sat unmoving, telling herself over and over again, 'My husband will take me away . . . I only have to wait . . . '

My husband: when at last she was left alone with him in the big bedchamber, Ko-chin was almost too tired to care what he thought of her. Trying to straighten her aching back, she stood with eyes fixed on his black velvet slippers, enduring his silent scrutiny. If only it had been allowed for her to speak first—to pour out her gratitude to this stranger who had stooped to save her, promise him he would never regret his kindness! But a woman's role was flower-like silence, downcast eyes, endless humility before her lord and master. Again Ko-chin felt a hot gush of anger from some newly opened spring deep within her—a spring that this young man's pity had unsealed: when at last he spoke, what she heard drove all memory of flower-like silences from her mind. This could not be true—that he was apologizing to her? Regretting that this marriage had been the only solution he could find in so short a time. When, for himself, he had sworn, 'I would never marry in the old way.'

'But what other way is there?' she cried in bitter shock. 'We have no choice!'

'Of course we do!' his voice snapped back. 'And, if we are to share our lives, little wife, choosing is something you must learn how to do.'

Ko-chin gave a choked sob; she might have known it—he was mad. So much for the change in her fortune. Desolately she turned her face away, eyes shut against the horror of her future, which could no more be avoided than his hostile womenfolk tomorrow. But she drew a sharp breath when she felt him step close, to lay a light finger on her cheek before he went on quietly, 'Little wife, there is much else besides you will need to learn, all of it contrary to what your mother has taught you. First of all, when I speak to you, I expect you to look me in the eyes.' Then, sounding almost as if it displeased him, he added abruptly, 'Your skin—it is like satin . . . '

At that, Ko–chin, warmed by the tenderness of his touch however outrageous the things he said, took courage. She raised her eyes to his face and knew at once that, whatever else he might be, this young man was not mad. His features were refined, his eyes intelligent, his mouth gentle—maybe her uncle was not so singular amongst men as she had thought. But her uncle did not have the shining warmth of this young man—could it really be that he was a new kind of person, part of that great change in the world of which her uncle had spoken?

But even as she began to smile, he broke their gaze and paced impatiently across the room, telling her in a voice suddenly cold, 'Wife, in Peking where we shall live, you must know that I belong to the Reform Club. Its members are committed to destroying the manacles of the past to set our country on the road to a happier future. The first step on that road for you and I is to change ourselves, reform our own thinking—'

There was more of the same but Ko-chin was no longer listening. How was she to win his heart, when he was so rapt in his vision of an impossible future? But at least she would not allow herself to be forgotten on this wedding night! She rallied her wits to seize his attention again. 'My lord,' she murmured the next time he paused for breath, 'you say that my mother's teaching is of no use to me as your wife. Guide me, I beg you: is it now a fault in me that I should believe my husband's wish to be my command?'

Han-lao swung round to stare down into her carefully solemn face and for the first time she saw him smile as, with equally deliberate care, he replied, 'There, honourable wife, I give you leave to use your discretion.'

Ko-chin bowed her head respectfully but on the way managed a mischievous sidelong look and this time he laughed aloud. His doubts about this doll-like creature thrust into his life suddenly forgotten, he declared, 'Little wife, I am happy that you have come to me! Although whether you too can be happy, living as I wish us to live, I do not know yet. When I do, then there will be time for other things between us—for now, I shall return to my own room. Sleep well.' And swiftly he turned on his heel and left her.

'But, my husband—'

It was too late, he had gone. Ko-chin gazed with stricken eyes at the still swaying door-curtain. How could she hope to win him if he would not share her bed? Or make sons? Tear-blinded she stumbled through the bed curtains and threw herself down. A bridal bed of richly carved rosewood with scarlet outer curtain, soft cream silk inner curtains fastened back on silver hooks; red satin pillows embroidered with birds and flowers; a satin coverlet strewn for the wedding night with rose petals and baby shoes: all she lacked was the bridegroom. There was nothing to do but sleep.

When Ko-chin awoke the lamp was burning low. Dowsing her face in cool water from the porcelain basin glazed with the lovely 'sky blue after the passing of rain', she began to think. Blue, it was the perfect colour: so what would a reformer like Han-lao consider to be a perfect wife? 'Because although he says he wants me to learn to choose,' she whispered to the shadowy room, 'if I do not seem happy making the choices he wishes me to make, then he will not choose me! So, to be kept with him, I must obey him just as wives have always obeyed their husbands, but make him believe I act of my own free will . . . '

It wouldn't be easy but Ko-chin had never expected life to be easy. She could do it, she told herself fiercely, huddling back under the padded quilt. But, oh, how much simpler it would be if, in the old way, she only had to make sons! Now, first, she must pretend that she wanted to be part of this strange new world being born in far-away Peking, that had so ensnared Han-lao. Only when she had remade herself to his pattern would he give her sons.

CHAPTER 3

CITY OF THE CELESTIAL EMPIRE

Next morning, two young wives frowned as Ko-chin entered the room but Mrs Li, splendid in black brocaded satin, remained intent on the servant lighting the tiny tobacco ball for her pipe. Only when she had taken several deep puffs did she turn to the trembling alien in her household to ask harshly, 'Is my son well pleased this morning, girl?'

'I—I do not know, ancient and honourable one,' Ko-chin stammered.

Mrs Li reached to slap her sharply on each cheek, spitting, 'And how should you, worm, when my son's bridal bed stayed cold?'

Ko-chin writhed: that everyone should know her shame and two here, at least, revelling in it . . . one of the young wives sneered now, 'Maybe a "reformer" does not know what a woman is for?'

But she had gone too far. Mrs Li whipped round on her, snarling, 'Dare you speak so in my presence? Leave me alone with this—this—'

She failed to find a word bad enough before the two girls had scuttled from the room and sank back into her chair, half her venom spent. Then she muttered, 'Come nearer, you. Ai ya! Know, wretch, that your coming into this house has shortened my years. Too late my poor son has seen his error! How will he give me grandsons now?'

The desolation in her voice was like a low-toned bell and Ko-chin, peeping swiftly upward, saw tears on the white cheeks. Truly, this woman suffered and Ko-chin's first instinct was to comfort. Coming a step closer she pleaded, 'Most honourable one, I beg you to forgive me—believe that I wish to do all in my power to please you!'

'Please me!' Mrs Li cried. 'How could such a one as you please me? Or my son either . . . Ai-ya! What can it be that my dearly loved fourth son lacks, that he even envies foreign devils their wicked follies! And worse, wishes to make our country copy them!'

Overwhelmed by horror at this new revelation, Ko-chin forgot respect. 'But foreign devils are monsters,' she gasped. 'How can it be that your son admires them?'

There was a fraught pause between them, then Mrs Li drew a long breath, a new gleam in her eyes. 'Ah, so there is some sense in you, girl,' she said grimly. 'Then maybe even yet you may make recompense: I command you to bring my son back to the ways of our people, as commanded by our great teacher Confucius! Remember, worm, absolute obedience to the Emperor, complete submission to your husband, and his submission to his father! Upon those principles our state is founded—a state civilized when foreign devils lived like monkeys!'

Contempt scalded in her voice which Ko-chin, blinded with tears, knew was as much for her as for foreign devils. How could she ever explain to this arrogant, ignorant woman that, if she were to obey her husband, the first casualty would be the iron grip of Confucius? For already Han-lao had told her that she, a mere woman, must learn to choose rather than to obey . . . and she did not think that, if the Emperor's wishes went against what his Reform Club wanted, Han-lao would obey even him. And what would happen then? Death by slicing was the fate of traitors . . .

Mrs Li ignored her choking sobs. 'First of all, of course, you must bring him to your bed,' she ordered. 'And since such a creature as you can hardly have been taught how best to do that, I must instruct you myself.'

And instruct she did. There was no pity in Mrs Li's heart for this intruder: for two full hours she kept Ko-chin swaying on bunched feet that turned to flame as she detailed rules Ko-chin had known since childhood—decorating her hair with jewels and flowers, painting her lips and finger nails correctly, preparing and presenting tea, listening in silence when her husband or an elder spoke, whether in praise or blame; when to play the harp and sing; the whole gentle art of seduction.

Then in loving detail Mrs Li described all Han-lao's favourite dishes—'For often, when he is tired or worried, he will refuse to eat and then you must coax him so that his strength does not fail.'

At the end, Ko-chin gasped, 'All this I will do, most honoured one, I swear it,' and knew that she lied. For whatever else she did not know, she knew that Han-lao did not want such a wife. What he did want she must find out, and soon, if ever she was to escape his dreadful mother.

But how, when for days she did not see Han-lao? When no one spoke to her, save the servant who, every evening, was sent to dress her hair in case her husband should deign to visit her bed? After the third day, Ko-chin swallowed her pride and asked the servant where Han-lao was.

'Oh, lady,' gabbled the girl, 'every day he visits his old school friends to tell them of the mad ideas he has brought back from the great city—such terrible things he says, the whole town is scandalized!'

She picked up a jewelled hairpin and Ko-chin interrupted, 'That is not mine,' and, watching the rich gold-set cornelian glow in the candlelight, added sadly, 'I have nothing so lovely.'

'Then be sure it is your husband's gift, lady,' declared the servant, 'for here it lay, ready to my hand.' And when, for the first time in this house, she saw Ko-chin's lips lift at the corners, she cried, 'How lovely my lady is when she smiles! When the young lord sees you thus, and in the new gowns I packed for you today, he will mend his ways!'

'New gowns—packed?' cried Ko-chin. 'So my husband is taking me with him to the city?'

'Never doubt it, lady—he is not so indifferent as he seems when he is still under his mother's eye. But in the house of his uncle and aunt in the city, it will be another matter.'

Ko-chin fervently hoped so and so, too, to judge by his farewell to his son, did Mr Li: 'Ah, my son, you went from us in your heart long ago, and now your body follows. Give us grandsons, that we may fill the void you leave behind you!'

Then Ko-chin was alone with her husband in the cart that was to carry them so far away from his home with its age and beauty, its flowering courtyards and luxurious furniture. 'Sons!' snorted Han-lao as their cart jolted away the first li of the long journey north. 'When will my honourable father understand that we reformers have to devote all our energies to saving our motherland? Had it not been for your plight, I would not even have married.'

For all the warmth of the early autumn day, Ko-chin felt cold to her core. If he wanted no sons, of what use was she? But Han-lao's spirits were too high for him to notice Ko-chin's frozen silence as any different from her usual modesty. Smiling down at her, he coaxed, 'This is our land, my wife—will you not look around you, instead of at your lap?'

Reluctantly Ko-chin peeped at the open fields—then upward to the great, unwalled sky. With a gasp of horror she clapped her hands to her eyes, crying, 'Oh, how terrible—we will be lost!'

Han-lao stared. Then he exclaimed, 'I had forgotten—you have never been outside before! But I promise you, little wife, you will soon rejoice in sunlight and air and your new freedom to travel through them!'

Rejoice? When her ears and eyes, used only to small, enclosed spaces, were being assailed by a whirling kaleidoscope of noise and colour, with never a moment's stillness to collect her wits? More likely she would go mad . . . At night Ko-chin plummeted into leaden sleep but every dawn heralded more roaring rivers, eye-stunning panoramas, squalid villages where listless children, bellies swollen with hunger, wrung her heart—and she had thought her own fate hard. But worst of all was Han-lao's relentless voice, refusing to let her shut out what she saw and heard, hammering into her stunned mind the facts and figures of their country's vast despair.

In the end, it was something that he did rather than all he said that helped her understand him better. At a grubby little wayside inn, a table had been set for them with rice and saucers of pickled cucumber, bean curd, red salted turnip, and sweet potatoes. Ko-chin grimaced as she tasted the tea but it rinsed her parched mouth and she had just picked up her chopsticks when a gasping coolie with a huge load on his back staggered in and, even as Han-lao ran to help him, collapsed on to the dirt floor. Ko-chin looked away. Coolie—that meant 'bitter strength'; so why should Han-lao soil his silk robe kneeling beside him to demand, 'Why risk killing yourself with such a load?'

'I am paid by the weight, lord,' the man croaked. 'Carry less, I earn less—and my family starves.' Then, after a rasping breath, he added, 'For the likes of us, lord, it's work or die. And the rich make sure we die working!'

Ko-chin's eyes widened indignantly. Surely Han-lao would not endure that? But he only muttered, 'I know how rich exploit poor in this land. But, believe me, there are some of us trying to alter that.'

Angrily the coolie pushed aside his supporting arm. 'Would you take even my work from me, young lord?' he demanded hoarsely, and struggled to his feet to heave up his load again.

Han-lao was silent the rest of the day and covertly Ko-chin watched him, her world suddenly back in focus. So, this husband of hers was not so strong in himself as she had thought. So open to the pain of others, he was deeply vulnerable. No wonder he had been unable to leave her to old Chen. Now it was her turn to help him, by distracting his thoughts . . . yet it was hard to break her mother's rule and be the first to speak. Just above a breath she murmured, 'My lord, the world grows bigger around us every day. How can it be that we shall ever find our destination?'

Startled out of his thoughts, Han-lao looked at her blankly for a moment, then his eyes warmed. 'That is the first time you have spoken to me of your own accord, wife,' he said softly and Ko-chin steeled herself for sarcasm: men never wanted their wives' opinions, let alone their thoughts interrupted. But, no, suddenly he was smiling: she had done the right thing, if only by mistake. Perhaps she could learn to be a reformer's wife after all . . . ?

But when at last, trundling across the great northern plain, she glimpsed for the first time the grey walls of Peking, capital of the Celestial Empire, looming against the horizon, panic overwhelmed her and she clung to the warm fingers Han-lao offered as he teased, 'Trembling like this, you remind me of the old emperor who told visitors from foreign lands that he expected them to "tremblingly obey"!'

Ko-chin managed a weak smile and whispered, 'And our own Emperor himself lives there in that city?'

'Like a pearl in an oyster—secretly in its heart,' Han-lao chuckled. 'Those walls ahead are only the first defence, guarding the area where the likes of you and I must live: that's in the Chinese City. Beyond and within, a second wall encircles the city of the Manchus, who have been our rulers ever since they rode down from the wild northern wastes of Manchuria—two cities, two races and, in the centre like a nut inside its shell, the wall of the Imperial City encloses the kernel: the Forbidden City, where the Emperor lives with all his eunuchs and women.'

Ko-chin, too absorbed now to remember courtesy, gasped, 'How beautiful it must be there, my husband!'

'Yes,' he said softly, remembering the richness of vermilion walls and golden yellow roofs. 'Especially you would like the carved dragons curling and writhing over the marble pavements.'

'It sounds very wonderful,' whispered Ko-chin, 'but we—we shall be living in the outer, Chinese City?'

'Yes, for our Manchu overlords do not care to mix too closely with mere Chinese.' Han-lao frowned, brooded for a while, then burst out, 'And this—' He seized his pigtail, the queue that reached halfway down his back, '—this is the symbol of my obedience to them—without a queue, any male older than fourteen years is guilty of high treason. Did you know that?'

It had never so much as occurred to Ko-chin to wonder why men wore queues. They just did. Was everything to have some hidden meaning from now on? She frowned and Han-lao chuckled, 'So you didn't! I thought not! Though not all Manchus are ogres, little wife: one here in Peking is my best friend and—'

But for the first time Ko-chin was not hanging on his every word. 'Oh, husband, what is happening?' she squeaked as their cart plunged into the dark tunnel through the wall's towering guardhouse. And on the other side of the wall, it was another world and Ko-chin, her mouth a round O of amazement, shrank close to Han-lao's side. Every other shock of the past days paled into insignificance beside her horrified fascination at the turmoil of men, sedans, camel trains, wheelbarrows, handcarts that seethed around them. A forest of signs—gold, blue, emerald—tall wooden pillars streaming with coloured flags—stalls heaped with furs—quack doctors thrusting bottles of Leaping Tiger Tonic and Snake Potion at passers-by—all mingling with the smells of roasting meat, soy, garlic, ginseng, and the stench of raw sewage. And everywhere beggars, knocking their pieces of wood together, pressing against their cart, pleading alms from a man rich enough not to walk.

'Have they no homes, no one to care for them?' Ko-chin cried.

'No one,' Han-lao shouted above the hubbub and Ko-chin closed her eyes. So this was what happened to people without strong sons to care for them. Better to endure the rigours of family life, however harsh your mother-in-law . . .

Han-lao's aunt, though, was not like his mother. Soft-spoken but, Ko-chin sensed, wholly in command not only of her household but herself. She glowed like a flower in her rose-hued gown as she led them through the courts and passageways of the great house. And to such an apartment—Ko-chin could not hold back an exclamation of delight when she saw it. Her own little courtyard, with a pool and a rockery set with dwarfed plum trees! Comfort everywhere and even a small annex where she could cook—for, Mrs Li explained, although they would often eat with the family, Han-lao kept irregular hours with his work and entertained many friends so, 'you will not always wish to eat with the family.'

That was puzzling; was she supposed to eat alone in the little annex, instead of joining the family for meals when Han-lao's friends called, Ko-chin wondered. Mrs Li smiled at her and, as soon as Han-lao had left them to rejoin his uncle, murmured, 'There must be many changes in the life of a reformer's wife, child. You will not find it easy to become one of the "new women", I fear. But remember this, I am always here to help and advise you. Come to me as you would to your own mother.'

'Oh!' Ko-chin fell to her knees, stammering her gratitude. Then she added, just above a whisper, 'And—and now, honourable lady, I understand why my husband feels this house to be his true home! I will be honoured to serve you.'

But Mrs Li said gently, 'You will have no tasks to do for me, little one. It is your husband who must guide your life here. Please me by pleasing him.'

'In everything I shall do my very best, most honourable one, to become what my husband wishes,' Ko-chin breathed.

'What other choice do you have?' the soft voice murmured. 'Tell me, child, is all as it should be between you?' Then she smiled as Ko-chin's cheeks flamed. 'I see it is not—as yet. Knowing a little of reformers, that does not surprise me as it does you. But remember, child, few men can live by ideals alone and one day he will be yours. And, although you must let him choose the time, you may mould events. Your weakness will be your strength, remember—but, who knows, one day you may prove to be the stronger.'

With these puzzling words Mrs Li left Ko-chin alone and, as the silence deepened around her, she gradually became aware of the weight of the centuries that had seen this great house grow like a living thing. Already it had absorbed herself and Han-lao, two more links in the long chain of men and women who had passed their lives within its walls. How could a way of life that spanned countless generations be changed by a few young men, however zealous? Here, Han-lao's ideas seemed crazier than ever.

CHAPTER 4

MANCHU

When Han-lao returned, Ko-chin hurried to make tea but he told her abruptly, 'The servant will do that, wife. I want to talk to you. You must understand that when we are not with the family you need not be formal with me. Here in our own rooms, we are friends and equals, and none of that nonsense about women hiding away when my friends call either, since they will regard you as I do—as just another reformer.'

Ko-chin stared in horror. 'But—my dear lord,' she stammered, 'I beg you—take thought for my reputation in your uncle's house! I cannot meet your friends!' Then, at his sudden frown, she added frantically, 'At least do not make me meet them yet—'

'I will "make" you do nothing,' Han-lao told her sternly. 'I am not commanding you as my wife: I am asking you as my co-worker: Ko-chin, will you meet the friends who will call to see me?'

She nodded dumbly, not daring to do anything else. With shaking hands she poured the tea the servant brought, knowing that at the very first hurdle she had shaken his trust in her. In desperation to make amends she resorted to flattery: 'My husband, you must be very clever, to have won a government position here in the capital city . . . '

'Not really,' he said shortly. 'Just born with a very good memory and a very rich father. They say, wife, that a government career is open to rich and poor alike but that is nonsense. It can take over ten years to learn what a man needs to know to pass the Imperial examinations. How many poor men's sons have that kind of leisure? It is high time they were replaced.'

'But by what, my lord?' asked Ko-chin timidly. 'What else can there be to learn?'

'Useful things,' cried Han-lao, cheeks flushing as he leant earnestly towards her, 'a whole world of knowledge, wife, of which we Chinese know nothing! The kind of knowledge which has shown the Westerners how to travel across the world to do as they please in our land! Now our only choice is to become as modern—as scientific—as they are or let them rape our entire country unhindered—' He broke off abruptly. 'But I go too fast for you, wife, forgive me.'

'I am too stupid,' she whispered, trying to hold back the scalding tears of humiliation. She did not even know what 'scientific' meant.

'Of course you are not,' Han-lao told her briskly. 'Why, you can already read and that's half the battle won.' His voice died away as he saw her face suddenly transformed.

'So I can,' she whispered, 'and to read is such an escape—the mind travels and leaves all else behind!'

Han-lao swallowed hard; for a moment there, he had glimpsed, instead of the usual frightened creature with no face of her own, a vibrant young woman. More startled than he liked to admit to himself, and more sharply than he meant, he demanded, 'Tell me then, wife, how many characters can you read?'

The light went from her eyes. 'Only three or four thousand at most, lord,' she faltered. 'There was so little time and it would not have done for our father to know we were being taught . . .'

'Then we must begin work at once, since you need at least seven thousand to read the newspapers,' began Han-lao grimly but, glimpsing her appalled face, he recovered himself and began to laugh. 'Cheer up, little wife,' he declared in his usual voice for her, 'after that there are only about another thirty-three thousand left to learn! Tell the servant to fetch rice paper, inkstone, water, and brushes and we will begin at once.'

They worked until it was time for the family's evening meal; then Ko-chin went to the women, Han-lao to the men, so that she sat amidst strangers in the flaring candlelight. The odours of baked fish and brown duck were fragrant upon the air as servants set bowls of vegetables and steaming rice along the tables, scattering chopsticks as they went. No one took any notice of her but she was still too petrified to eat more than a few mouthfuls. As soon as she could, she crept back to the quiet of their own apartment to practise her new characters.

Han-lao did not return. Alone in the big bed, she heard, as though the woman stood by her side, her mother-in-law's parting words: 'Dare not return to this house, girl, still barren!'

'Can I help it if he cares more for how well I write than for how well I look?' she cried aloud into the darkness. 'Oh, Kuan-yin, help me!'

Next evening when Han-lao returned from his work, Ko-chin was ready; the subtle fragrance of water-lilies wafted from her silken hair, the sheen of her green satin gown fell smoothly to her tiny feet in black velvet shoes sewn with gold beads. But he hardly glanced at her. At last, in desperation, she allowed her hand to brush against his as she passed his tea bowl and faltered, 'Was—was your first day in your new office not pleasing to you, lord?'

Han-lao raised stormy eyes. 'It was not, wife,' he snapped and subsided again into brooding silence.

Now was the moment, Ko-chin told herself agonizedly, when a proper wife would be able to comfort him. Gathering together all her courage, she stretched a hand towards him but she was too late: footsteps and voices sounded outside and Han-lao's face cleared like magic.

'Sung,' he exclaimed, 'my friend the Manchu prince of whom I told you, wife.'

But Ko-chin only had time to catch sight of the large booted feet of their visitor before she fled. When, a moment later, Han-lao followed her to the annex he found her crouched in a corner, scarlet with shame. Gently he rested a hand on her bent head. 'Do not upset yourself, wife,' he whispered. 'I have spoken to Sung. Tonight we are agreed you shall sit behind the curtain, where you can hear what is said without being seen by the other members of the Reform Club when they arrive.'

Ko-chin's eyes dazzled in the soft light as she raised her face to him, choking, 'How good you are to me, husband!' and she meant it. Even so, it was horribly hard to sit so close to male voices and laughter; did they know she was there, a small interloper listening to all they said? Were other young women in this city being forced to do such things? Or were they like her husband, free of spirit and contemptuous of the only rules she knew to live by? Ko-chin tried to calm her pounding heart and concentrate. Who was this 'Pearl Concubine' they spoke of? As for the Emperor's aunt—Ko-chin shivered as she heard, 'They say that, as a child, every time the Emperor saw his aunt he screamed for help! Small wonder, then, that even now at twenty-eight years old he dares do nothing without her consent.'

'Yet, if we are to have our way, we must find a way to give him the courage to defy her,' came another voice, very deep and firm. Was that Han-lao's friend, the Prince Sung, Ko-chin wondered.

Someone laughed scornfully. 'Why, he cannot even save his precious Pearl Concubine from a beating if his aunt commands it! And I tell you again, since his aunt knows as well as we do that that girl is our best hope of winning the Emperor to command the reform movement, she will do her best to drive the Pearl to suicide.'

'But while the Pearl Concubine lives she will smuggle the books to him that we want him to read,' broke in Sung's deep voice again. 'He's no fool, for all he might sometimes seem it. Nowadays, books on all the sciences as well as law and the foreign political systems are grist to his mill and every new idea he absorbs works in our favour—although we can hardly expect him to agree with what foreigners call "democracy"!'

'But until we can put those other new ideas into practice we are helpless—' That was Han-lao's voice; Ko-chin glowed and pressed her cheek against the curtain.

'As our Imperial government intends we should be, in case we endanger its own important self,' broke in a new voice, potent with malice. 'Oh, I know, after the Japanese, because they'd modernized, managed to steal lands from our Empire a few years ago, there was a great hubbub about modernizing ourselves—but has that stopped the foreigners carving up our country between them like a water-melon? I tell you again, it is the spinelessness of the Manchus that holds us back at every turn and, whatever gentlemen like our friend Han-lao here would have us believe, we need violent means to get rid of both them and the foreigners—not weak-kneed reforms on paper! There's no choice but to use violence to get our way!'

'You say this, Ting-i, and—' began Sung's deep voice, but now the man called Ting-i turned on him, shouting, 'Am I the only one not allowed to give my opinion, Manchu?'

Ko-chin shuddered again; so this man hated her husband's friend as well as her husband—and she had thought the reformers were all on the same side. She frowned as Sung actually agreed with the worm! Could he really be saying, 'I was about to confirm that opinion, Ting-i. Because there's no doubt in my mind either that, in the end, we will have to use violence. My friend Han-lao forgets the peasants' loathing for the foreign devils who force us to import the goods that are wrecking their livelihoods. To say nothing of the foreign godmen, insisting their converts aren't subject to Chinese law, so that Chinese Christians can literally get away with murder! Oh, it's all right for us, Han-lao, to talk about gradual change but we can't expect peasants watching their families die of hunger to see things the same way.'

So, thought Ko-chin, her uncle had been right: a great storm was brewing. That night she tossed and turned between the soft coverlets of the bed; never in her life before had she heard so much talk and her over-stimulated brain could not relax. When at last she did fall into a restless doze, the tall figure of the mysterious Manchu girl called the Pearl Concubine haunted her dreams.

CHAPTER 5
LISTENING BEHIND SCREENS

For the next few days Han-lao was too busy to see much of Ko-chin, but he left her such lists of new characters to learn that she had a permanent headache and no spare time for plans to lure him to her bed. At least, though, he had said no more about meeting his friends face to face. Ko-chin's jaw set as she watched him sip his favourite Dragon Well tea one evening, while he checked her day's characters: anything else she would do, but not that.

It was as if he had read her thoughts. Pushing aside the closely written sheets, he smiled, 'You are a swift learner, little wife—these are excellent. Now, please me even further: tomorrow night my friend the Prince Sung comes to dine and I wish him to meet my wife for more than a few seconds this time!' He gave her his most shining smile but Ko-chin stared in such frozen misery that he stuttered a little as he went on. 'And—and I wish you to look as beautiful as you did then, wife . . . '

So he had noticed, but small use it had been to her. Rebellion stirred in Ko-chin's heart: she would take this to Mrs Li.

Seeing her face set, Han-lao fought down his impatience; if he hated her usual submissiveness, it was hardly reasonable to be annoyed when she did show some signs of willpower of her own. But making her understand took precious spare time, time he should be spending on his English exercises; a pity that such an appallingly difficult language should be so necessary to a modern man . . . Han-lao sighed heavily and jerked his mind back to his more immediate problem, this wife of his—exactly the kind of distraction a reformer did not need. 'My wife,' he began, with another, heavier sigh, 'my friend Sung is one of the few Manchus—who, don't forget, rule us—on the side of the reformers at the moment. We need him desperately, and he will be hugely impressed if he finds an untaught Chinese girl with the courage to break the mould of her life for our cause. So will all the other reformers, of course, although—'

He hesitated and Ko-chin, glancing up at his suddenly uneasy face, remembered the reformer Ting-i's high-pitched, venomous voice. 'Although not all reformers wish for Manchus to work with us, husband?' she questioned stiffly.

He seized her hands in his and for a moment her heart leapt. But it was his friend's cause he was pleading, not his own: 'I tell you, wife,' he declared passionately, 'there are good men everywhere! Sung may belong by blood to the race that misrules us, but that does not stop him believing that misrule is wrong—and trying to do something about it!'

'But how can he work against his own people?' cried Ko-chin.

'Because, like me, he believes that all men are broth-ers—that no just government allows thousands of its people to die for lack of food.' Han-lao dropped her hands and stared at her accusingly. 'Have you forgotten already the beggars you saw in the streets of Peking?'

Stung, she retorted, 'I have not, but has the Emperor seen them?'

'Of course not, but he has been told,' Han-lao snapped back, 'but as yet he is too afraid of his aunt and her army allies to agree to our reforms. While we try to win the Emperor, Sung plays a double game: the Manchus think he spies on us for them—in reality it is the other way round.'

Ko-chin was appalled. 'But, my husband,' she cried, 'the Emperor's aunt—her armies—if it comes to blows, he must betray us if only for his family's sake . . . '

Han-lao's face darkened in outrage. 'Sung would do no such thing!' he snapped. 'Understand that once a man is a reformer even the good of his family takes second place to the good of his country. The whole point of what we are doing is to make everyone's lives—rich or poor, man's or woman's—worth living and secure against foreign take-over. That won't be achieved by half-heartedness. It's all or nothing, Ko-chin. You do understand that, don't you?'

Ko-chin nodded meekly but only because when she had spoken her mind he had become angry. Inside, though, she felt anything but meek because, for the first time in her life, she considered she had a right to her own opinion: and that opinion was that no one should sacrifice his own family's interests for something so stupidly abstract as a 'country'—and how would the Prince Sung's father, mother, wife feel if he were to die the traitor's agonizing death-by-slicing? Understand indeed!

The next morning, still buoyed up by indignation, Ko-chin took her problems to Mrs Li. 'The most honourable lady said that this unworthy one might come to her for advice,' she began with unusual confidence and Mrs Li smiled down at the meekly bowed head that did not match the voice.

'Indeed I did,' she replied serenely. 'But understand, your husband's cause is so close to the hearts of my husband and myself that I am unlikely to give you advice that goes against his wishes!'

Ko-chin's own heart plummeted: 'But, honourable lady,' she cried, 'there are some things that cannot in decency be done! I must tell you that my husband wishes me to display myself like a flower girl before his men friends! That would dishonour this house—'

'My nephew holds this house in all honour, child,' Mrs Li interrupted, 'as he does you, if you would but believe it. So far, all the changes that he has brought into your life have been to your clear benefit, have they not? Would you then fail him at the first hard thing he asks of you in return?'

Ko-chin flushed. 'I know of his goodness to me, honourable one,' she muttered, 'and I would gladly give him sons in return, if he would only share my bed!'

'But, little one, it is not sons he wants at present,' said Mrs Li softly, 'and you have more than enough to do learning how to become a reformer's wife, as I think you well know. So tell me, what is it that really bothers you so much about meeting the Prince Sung—for that, we know, is all that my nephew requires of you this night.'

But was it? If only she could believe that . . . with a gasp Ko-chin covered her face with her hands, wailing, 'Oh lady, this husband of mine does not even seek to please his honourable mother! So how little will he care for me? I fear that, not wanting me himself, tonight he gives me to his friend!'

Her latest terror spoken aloud, all the others of the past weeks overwhelmed her: Ko-chin forgot respect, self-restraint, and sank in a crumpled heap to the floor. Mrs Li let her weep and, when the storm had passed, summoned a servant with hot towels to wipe Ko-chin's drenched face, saying quietly, 'Ko-chin, you must know that if you fail this test you will surely be sent back—childless—to the courts of your mother-in-law. Is that what you really want?'

Ko-chin stumbled to her feet and took the hands that Mrs Li stretched towards her, choking, 'Most honourable lady, I see that I must obey my husband and meet the Prince Sung this night.'

A soft, scented palm patted her damp cheek. 'Give each such obedience the grace of consent, my dear, whether or not you feel it, and I think your husband's defences against you will crumble soon enough. So, return now to your apartment and prepare yourself to please him in every way.'

If only it was that simple . . . but Han-lao's face was very easy to read and Ko-chin knew, as soon as he returned that evening, that far from finding her desirable in her best finery, he saw only a cleverly fashioned doll cluttering his apartment and his life. Never had Ko-chin felt so inadequate before, but she could not say the words of reassurance that would break the chill silence between them. Tension as tight as the bandages that held her broken feet gripped her throat, killing speech. But not her thoughts: what a tale their servant would have to tell tomorrow morning . . . her reputation in this house would be ruined. But that didn't matter any more, just so long as Han-lao did not send her away.

Han-lao was handsome in his best deep-plum satin gown and sleeved black satin jacket, but his usually mobile face was very still as, waiting for Sung, his eyes brooded on Ko-chin. In soft green satin, with jade in her ears and in the silk-netted knot of her hair, tiny feet in flowered satin shoes, she could have stepped from some ancient picture. Had her upbringing ensured that she was no more than a copy, or was there a living being with a will of her own inside that carefully perfect shell? Was he only tormenting her—and himself—keeping her here with him, when by nature she was only fitted for the old style of life in his mother's courts? Well, tonight would tell . . .

Taller than any Chinese, broad, vigorous, with an aura of magnetic energy that set the quiet room tingling, the Prince Sung strode into their apartment, thick-soled boots resounding as Han-lao's black velvet indoor shoes never did: Ko-chin, devastated, fled.

In the kitchen she stood alone, gulping deep breaths of air fragrant with the aromas of baked fish and duck-filled pancakes. Then, desperately collecting her scattered wits, she remembered to send the servant with hot towels so that the two men could wipe their hands and faces before eating. When the meal was over, Han-lao would call her; she must not fail him—or herself—again.

It was change or die, Ko-chin told herself fiercely, clutching at the table edge. Useless to believe there was any safety in clinging to past ways, or aid in her mother's training; she had only her own small reserves of courage and intelligence with which to create a different future—now.

When she was called, Ko-chin went without hesitation to receive Sung's congratulations on an excellent meal. And because, to please Han-lao even more, she had not dropped her eyes before him, she saw at once that he had no intention of insulting her—his face was carefully turned away. It was Han-lao who was staring! Ko-chin drew a long overdue breath and, with the sudden release of tension, nearly giggled. For once, at least, she had taken this clever husband of hers by surprise and that was very good for him!

Ko-chin swiftly dropped her eyes but not before Han-lao had glimpsed their sudden laughter. How dared she find him funny! With barely controlled annoyance he told her stiffly, 'Our friend Sung, understanding your difficulty, my wife, has brought this screen for you, so that you may listen unseen when I have visitors—'

'Just as the Emperor's aunt does herself in the Forbidden City!' Sung added, as Han-lao paused uncertainly.

With a tremulous smile at Han-lao, Ko-chin slipped behind it to the chair set ready for her. How wrong she had been to doubt this husband of hers; even his friend was kind . . . Ko-chin settled to listen and blushed at Sung's deep-throated chuckle as he declared, 'Your wife needs lessons in self-confidence from that old-time British ambassador who refused to kowtow to our Emperor. He had no intention of humbly knocking his head on the floor nine times in front of anyone!'

'But in those days our Emperors still believed that foreigners came to our land to pay us tribute,' said Han-lao. 'This history my wife still has to learn . . .'

At any other time that chill in his voice would have frozen Ko-chin's heart, but Sung's interruption diverted her: 'But instead of tribute they brought us opium,' he was saying harshly, all laughter gone from his voice, 'and with it gunboats to silence any objections we might make to its wholesale poisoning of our people. And, of course, they brought us their "all merciful god" as well, eager to welcome the opium addicts up into his heaven!'

Ko-chin heard Han-lao shift restlessly in his chair. 'We have more than their opium to worry us now,' he snapped. 'If we don't learn how to fight back on their own terms they will soon be toppling the Emperor from his throne and setting up camp in the Forbidden City!'

Ko-chin sat aghast behind her screen. Foreign devils? Creatures with fuzzy red or yellow wool for hair, huge noses, pale pebbles for eyes—pallid skins and feet like rice flails! 'Oh, Kuan-yin,' she sent up a hasty prayer, 'grant that I never have to see such a thing!'

Then she gasped. Sung was speaking to her! 'My friend's wife, let me ask you a question. How can we make soldiers good enough to drive the foreign devils from our land?'

'She cannot answer that!' cried Han-lao before Ko-chin could find her voice. 'There's no such thing as a good soldier—they are beasts, not men!'

'Tell that to the barbarians,' replied Sung calmly. 'It's only because they have such good soldiers that they can rape our country with no more than token opposition. Again, I ask your wife, why can't we make soldiers with enough backbone to defend our rights?'

And from behind the screen Ko-chin, seeing vividly in her mind's eye the plump features and petulant mouth of her brother, Huang, whispered, 'Because our boy children are treated like little gods and protected from every hardship. They never learn how to struggle against difficulties.'

'Who makes them grow up this way?' asked Sung tensely.

And Han-lao heard that small voice answer without hesitation, 'We women. Because in everything we submit to men; from birth they are denied nothing.'

'Exactly,' roared Sung, 'and so we have become a race of spoilt children, who fall apart at the first hint of trouble. Women's only power may be in their own homes, but it is real power: with it, they unman us!'

Ko-chin forgot every taboo in flaring anger. 'Power?' she cried. 'When we are taught that we women, being yin and creatures of Earth, are born to be passive? It is you men who make the world what it is, since you are yang, belonging to heaven which is full of movement! You act, we submit—that is the way of the universe.'

'It is,' Sung rapped back, 'but remember that, within itself, yang contains the seed of yin, and yin of yang; each is continually transforming itself into the other, but in this land of ours we have become such slaves to the past that we've forgotten how to change to meet changed circumstances—*that* is against the way of Nature. Small wonder our society sickens!'

Ko-chin raised her delicate brows. 'Then, lord,' she asked smoothly, 'are we women to tell men what to do for a time?'

And she smiled behind her concealing screen as Sung snapped, 'Of course not—what I am saying is, just because yin naturally gives way to yang, it does not mean it's right to imprison all yin creatures. It is no more good for anyone to be totally subservient, than for anyone to be completely satisfied. All extremes are bad.'

Ko-chin thought. Then she asked, 'Can it therefore be good for the Emperor to be all-powerful?'

Han-lao caught his breath. Could that really be his wife saying such things? Better she kept silent if those were the sort of things inside her head! 'That is too dangerous to think, let alone say,' he blurted but, to her own amazement as much as his, Ko-chin persisted—she felt safe behind this screen of hers:

'But, my husband, ignorant though I am, it seems to me that these things are the same: the women are shut away while the men are free; the rich and powerful have everything and the poor nothing.'

'She is right, my friend.' Sung's deep voice, from high above her head this time, had a tremor in it as he went on, 'We reformers have to talk as if our tinkerings could repair foundations which are rotten to the core. But say they collapse at the first hammer blow and come tumbling down about our heads? No more Emperor's aunt, but maybe no more Emperors either. A total breakdown of law and order as we know them—are we really prepared for that?'

'Of course not,' groaned Han-lao. 'We'd be like cockerels running round without their heads, leaving the field wide open for warlords and foreigners to do their worst.'

'Exactly, my friend,' said Sung grimly. 'Yet maybe that is our only way ahead. In the meantime, take good care of this little wife of yours. I suspect she is not so much a reformer in the bud as an infant revolutionary! And now I must bid you goodnight . . . '

He could not be leaving so soon! Ko-chin's hand flew to her mouth as she stumbled out from behind her screen. 'Oh, my husband,' she sobbed, 'I have driven away your guest when I only thought to please you by speaking out!' But, although her distress was genuine enough, she knew what she said was not entirely true because, as her brain had stretched to meet Sung's, she had forgotten not only herself but Han-lao too.

Han-lao shook his head numbly. Indifference—impatience—irritation—anger: he had felt them all towards this girl in the past few hours. But he could not bear to see her wretched. Swiftly he gathered her to him, telling himself he really did have at last what he had thought he wanted: a wife with a mind of her own. He just hadn't expected it to be quite so overwhelming an experience . . .

'My friend was not upset because he thought you had spoken out of turn,' he told her gently, 'but because what you said had only one possible answer from either of us. You see, my wife, both Sung and I are desperately afraid that the only way our country can really be changed is by all-out war.'

'War!' breathed Ko-chin. Was that what her uncle had meant by a great storm brewing? 'But, my husband, I thought the reformers were going to make things better for us! If there is war we women could not even run away!'

Han-lao bent and lifted her tiny foot. It fitted into the palm of his hand and Ko-chin waited for compliments that did not come. Instead, he just put her foot so gently back on to the floor that she felt nothing. But he had never smiled at her like that before and Ko-chin shivered with sudden joy as he murmured, 'Don't let's look too far into the future. I think that, at present, my most important reform is to free my own wife to speak and think and run.'

Ko-chin was too absorbed to notice his fleeting, downward glance at her feet as he went on, 'That is, of course, if now you know what is at stake you still choose to stay and help me with my work here. But if you would rather return to my father's house to live the life you expected . . . '

Ko-chin returned his intent gaze without fear or shame. 'My husband, I choose to stay with you. I do not always understand what you ask of me, but I trust you and wherever you lead I will follow—' She hid her face from him then, whispering through her fingers, 'My lord, all I beg of you is never to send me from you!'

Han-lao bent to rest his cheek against hers, breathing, 'That I promise!' Then, holding her away from him to stare down into her flushed face, his voice pealed triumphantly, 'Ko-chin, we are young, young, young. Together we cannot fail! We—and others like us—will bring all the old walls tumbling down!'

And echoing, 'Young, my lord!' Ko-chin lifted her hands to unpin her hair.

The scent of jasmine oil wafted about them and she trembled: she had crossed her first bridge, but there were so many others ahead—and men did not keep promises made to women in the heat of the moment; she needed far more to bind him to her. Surely—surely now he must take her to his bed! But it seemed an eternity before he stretched out a hand to stroke her shining, waist-long tresses, whispering, 'Yin and yang, man and woman, nothing is possible for either without the other, is it? Maybe I have been wrong to keep myself from you . . . '

Ko-chin said nothing, just stretched out to him her slender hands, the rosy-stained and scented palms held upward.

CHAPTER 6

'NEVER GRIEVE'

As autumn passed into winter pedlars brought hard yellow persimmons to the gates to sell, instead of glowing cherries; and, as the cold grew more bitter, Ko-chin shivered even in her fur-trimmed gowns. She was too happy in this new life of hers to care about that, though. It was only when she remembered how soon now Mo-ch'o must be sent to a husband that the old sense of hopelessness touched her. Girls were so helpless and given a father such as theirs . . .

Ko-chin shook herself: this was no way to think on today of all days—when she herself was to begin helping to change the world. Any moment now, she would be breaking the taboo against a Chinese woman meeting a Manchu woman—and not just any Manchu woman but the princess who was Sung's wife! What would this Lan-kuei be like? Ko-chin's stomach flipped with panic. Because, whatever Sung might say, she was sure his wife would hate being taught how to read and write Chinese characters by someone as humble as herself; and, anyway, Lan-kuei would have been reared despising Chinese . . .

Ko-chin groaned, then tried to pull herself together. Stupid to be afraid of a girl so little older than herself, she told herself fiercely. Lan-kuei might be Manchu, high-born to the master race, but the Pearl Concubine was Manchu too, and Ko-chin admired that shadowy figure more than any person she knew about. It was the Pearl who diced with death every day, finding ways to get the books and letters sent by the reformers to the Emperor past his terrible aunt's army of spies. So surely Ko-chin could deal with a mere princess—especially one who, although she was already sixteen years old, didn't have a son. In fact, by the time Lan-kuei had been sneaked into the house by its secret Gate of Peaceful Escape—'There in case the poor get tired of being hungry and storm the front gates of the rich,' according to Han-lao—she would have very little pride left!

But it seemed that Lan-kuei was made of sterner stuff than Ko-chin had hoped. Under its heavy mask of paint, the Manchu girl's face was so sullenly haughty that Ko-chin's warm greeting died on her lips. Her own simple gown of pink silk embroidered with plum blossoms, with only a spray of pearls to decorate her hair, felt ridiculously young and simple beside this stately figure's gorgeous gown and high-piled hair held by jewelled hairpins. But then Ko-chin glimpsed her guest's shoes: she had forgotten that Manchu women weren't allowed to bind their feet! Thank Heaven that, however unsophisticated she might look otherwise, she didn't have to wear shoes as big as a peasant's, with central heels a full six inches high to boot!

Suddenly aware of how she was staring, Ko-chin desperately tried to remember how this important guest should be greeted but the words wouldn't come. In the end, it was Lan-kuei who broke the silence between them. 'I must ask a favour of you, lady . . . ' she began harshly and Ko-chin gasped, 'I shall be most honoured, lady!'

Lan-kuei swept one scornful look over Ko-chin's slight figure, then, fixing her eyes on the floor, muttered, 'My husband wishes me to learn how to read and write Chinese and since it seems you have these skills . . . '

'I should be delighted to teach you the very little that I know,' Ko-chin finished stiffly for her and silence fell again.

She only came because her husband made her, thought Ko-chin resentfully. She isn't a true reformer, like him—she despises us Chinese, so why should she care what happens to our people? Courage flooding back, she lifted her head and delivered her challenge: 'Honourable lady, I fear the friendship that our husbands wish to see between us is distasteful to such a high one as yourself. I must assure you it is none of my unworthy seeking.'

Lan-kuei's dignity fled. Stumbling across to seize Ko-chin's hands she cried, tears smudging her eyes, 'Oh, don't be angry with me! I need a friend so terribly and only to you dare I speak the truth—that my husband has turned against his own people! If any of our own kind should guess . . . ' She gulped: to swallow her pride like this, and to a Chinese! But she couldn't go on alone any longer. 'I obey him, as I must,' she stumbled on, 'but you surely can guess how hard it is for me? I am no Pearl Concubine, to dice with dishonour and death!'

Disarmed, Ko-chin took the shaking girl's hands, telling her with a firmness that surprised herself, 'We must be friends for our own as well as our husbands' sakes, Lan-kuei. Now, will you not sit down at the table, where inkstone, brushes, and paper are ready? Between us we shall never write such a Letter of Ten Thousand Words as my husband has told me the reformers' leader K'ang wrote for the Pearl Concubine to smuggle to the Emperor; but at least soon, I promise you, there will be another Manchu lady who knows a Chinese character when she sees it!'

Drop by drop, she added water to the inkstone, mixing until she had a glistening black liquid in which to moisten the brushes. Then, as she had been taught herself, she began to teach Lan-kuei.

The time fled by. Just as Ko-chin was drawing breath to ask Lan-kuei whether she had ever seen the Pearl Concubine, she heard deep voices nearby and gasped instead, 'It will be your husband come home with mine! I must leave you, Lan-kuei.'

'Why so?' snapped Lan-kuei before she could stop herself. 'For you have met my husband face to face before this day, have you not?' Then, ashamed at the hurt in Ko-chin's eyes, she added swiftly, 'But well enough I know that was none of your doing. These husbands—always they find new ways to make their wives' lives more difficult!'

Taken aback at the bitterness in Lan-kuei's voice, Ko-chin was too late to escape Han-lao and Sung's arrival. Rubbing his hands from cold, Han-lao greeted Lan-kuei, then turned to Ko-chin declaring, 'A letter for you at last, little wife. News from your family home.'

Ko-chin swiftly bowed in Sung's direction and scuttled away with her precious letter. Eagerly she ran her eyes down her mother's characters, which were distorted with haste. Then she stumbled back to the room where Han-lao was congratulating Lan-kuei on her first characters. 'Oh, husband,' she cried, voice stark with anguish as she thrust the letter into his hands, 'my little sister—the fate you rescued me from has fallen upon her!'

Quickly Han-lao scanned the letter and, when Sung demanded, 'Tell me', he outlined for him the events that had led to his sudden marriage to Ko-chin. 'And now my wife's sister is to take her place,' he ended furiously. 'Oh, how it sickens me, this buying and selling of women—save one and another takes her place!'

Sung's wide-set eyes glittered. '"Another" may be saved too, if your wife allows me to help,' he said sharply, turning to Ko-chin. 'Tell me of the girl, my friend's wife.'

Stammeringly, Ko-chin told them about Mo-ch'o, her voice catching as she ended on a sob: 'If Mo-ch'o is given to that cruel old man she will take her life, I know it. Like so many girls who swallow their ear-rings or jump down wells rather than live the lives they have been given!'

'Mo-ch'o,' murmured Sung. 'That means "Never grieve". We must make sure she never does. Now, my friend's wife—' The clear blood mantling her cheeks, Ko-chin looked into his eyes as he told her, 'I have a friend without a wife who, as a boy, ran away to join the revolutionaries in the south. It may be he would wed your sister to save her.' He held up an impatient hand. 'I know, Han-lao, difficult to baulk old Chen a second time, and his son already swearing vengeance on you, but leave that to me.'

Mouth a little open, Ko-chin stared up at the hard, chiselled lines of this tall young man's face and understood why Lan-kuei seemed half afraid of him; it would not do to get in his way and she shivered as Han-lao said doubtfully, 'But first you must find your friend and even then . . .'

Sung only laughed. 'I know where he is—quite near by, as it happens. How else do you think I always know what the revolutionaries in the south are doing? And I know he will help because I know him. Come, wife, there is an urgent message to send.'

At once Lan-kuei stumbled after him on her impossible shoes but she smiled a goodbye to Ko-chin over her shoulder. The Chinese couple were left standing alone in the suddenly silent room. Then Han-lao smiled too as he took Ko-chin's hand. 'Do you believe now, my love, that in the new world we will make, all things are possible?'

And, eyes radiant, she smiled back at him, whispering, 'I do, my lord.'

Han-lao took a deep breath; was this the right moment, when she had just been shown so clearly how unselfish action could change the hardest of fates, to ask her to take her next step on the road to becoming one of the new women? Hesitatingly he began, 'As you learn yourself, Ko-chin, so soon you will be asked to help other women . . .'

'As I am your friend's wife?' asked Ko-chin a trifle smugly as, her terror for Mo-ch'o receding, she remembered her own life.

'Exactly! But sometimes in their homes rather than in yours.' Han-lao let that sink in, then went on carefully,

'And, who knows, one day my work may take us abroad, where you will certainly need to be able to walk more easily and further. So, little wife—I know it will be hard—but—' He swallowed, then blurted, 'I wish you to unbind your feet.'

Ko-chin could not believe her ears. He could not be serious! Unbind her lily feet, when having them bound had cost her such pain? After that long agony to let them spread like a peasant's? Never!

Han-lao scowled. 'Look at me, Ko-chin!' He lifted her chin in his hand but she would not raise her eyes and he knew he had struck that vein of rock in her character again. Coldly he went on, 'For even if you are proud of those misshapen horrors, wife, I hope you don't expect me to enjoy looking at them?'

Ko-chin winced. And she had thought her husband would be proud of her tiny feet in their pretty embroidered slippers, of her walk like a lily swaying in the wind . . . but she might have known. When did Han-lao ever think or do what was usual? It would be different when he was older and his reforming days only a memory, though. Bitterness scalding her throat, she said thickly, 'You say that now, husband, but if I obey you, how can I be sure that later you will not sicken at my ugliness and take a small-foot for a second wife!'

'You women!' Han-lao flared back. 'You treat us like gods but in your hearts you have utter contempt for us, don't you? Only the sons we give you really matter to you! So, look at it this way: how will your sons feel when they find out their mother refused to become a modern woman, even though their father gave her every chance?'

'My—my sons?' she faltered.

'Yes, those unborn sons to whom you have already given your heart, leaving no room for me,' Han-lao snapped; she might as well know she was not the only one who could feel bitter.

Ko-chin stared back at him numbly. How could he expect a husband to be what a son was to a woman? Husbands soon visited flower girls, took other wives and concubines: such they were, they could not help it. But a son had only one mother and her place was inalienable. What other real security was there for any woman in a world that otherwise called her worthless? But Han-lao really didn't seem to think that women were worthless—was she being unfair to him? Oh, it was all so muddling! Heaven knew she hated the way things were as much as he seemed to do, but—'Oh, my husband,' she whispered, 'do you not know how much it would hurt me to unbind my feet?'

Instantly he was beside her, voice very gentle as he urged, 'I do know and hate asking it of you! But only women like you, by your own example, can kill this hideous practice. Ko-chin, if the reformers can end foot-binding, we will save so many young girls the agony you suffered! Think of them when you choose to unbind your feet!'

'But I cannot care for all the world,' cried Ko-chin frantically. 'I will never see those girls, never know them! It is hard enough for a woman to take care just for herself and, if you are truly a reformer, you know you have surrendered the right to force any decision on me just because I am a woman and your wife!'

Even as she spoke, though, Ko-chin remembered the Pearl Concubine. There was one woman who, even though she was sealed within the Forbidden City with every luxury to hand, had chosen to care what happened to others less fortunate than herself . . . but even so, Ko-chin told herself fiercely, it wasn't natural and the eyes she raised to Han-lao were still full of defiance.

It was very satisfying to glimpse the shame in his eyes before he turned his face away, muttering, 'It's not so easy as that, Ko-chin. You—you are right, of course, but you must consider my position as well. When I married you, some of my friends thought I had failed as a reformer because they don't believe a married man can give his whole commitment to our cause.'

He broke off with a harsh laugh. 'And they're right, aren't they, because it shouldn't be this hard for me to command you to take your first step on to so painful a road—but I have to do it, Ko-chin, not just because I think it's right that you should but because I'll lose face if you don't. And so will you. I don't want anyone saying you're not a fit wife for me—'

'So you are telling me this cannot be my choice at all,' Ko-chin finished for him and, with a soft rustle of silk, left the room.

Han-lao sank into a chair, head in hands. Perhaps Mrs Li—or, better, Lan-kuei—would be able to make her see sense.

And so, when a few days later Lan-kuei came and Ko-chin burst out, 'Oh, my friend, my husband commands me to unbind my feet!' Lan-kuei replied calmly, 'And so, if he is a reformer, he should. You Chinese girls cannot go on being deliberately crippled to make you into playthings for men and fit for nothing else. Why, you cannot even run.'

Neither can you, in those shoes, thought Ko-chin rebelliously, although aloud she only said pointedly, 'I have heard that many Manchu women would bind their feet if the law allowed.'

Lan-kuei frowned. 'Maybe so, but that doesn't make it right. And I don't understand how you can grudge doing this for your husband when he has done so much for you.' Ko-chin had no answer to that and Lan-kuei, relishing this rare opportunity to feel in the right, added softly, 'Maybe, though, you wish your own daughters to have the Chinese women's chance to rekindle old men's lusts with their lily feet?'

Oh, but that was nasty! Ko-chin had suspected Lan-kuei to be jealous of her sometimes before but now she could not hide her amazed hurt. At last she muttered, 'I had thought you and I were friends, Lan-kuei . . . '

Lan-kuei's small shrug was eloquent—her, be friends with a Chinese girl?—and some inhibition deep inside Ko-chin's being suddenly snapped. Thoughts racing, she stared unseeingly at Lan-kuei. Manchus despised Chinese . . . rich despised poor . . . and men despised women—who, instead of uniting against all those oppressions, made them worse by spiteful divisions between themselves. If, by unbinding her feet, she could unlock a single link in that long chain of human misery, she would do it.

For the first time understanding a little of the compulsion that drove the Pearl Concubine to take such desperate risks, Ko-chin rose to her feet and smiled down into Lan-kuei's suddenly embarrassed face. 'If you will excuse me for a few moments, lady,' she said softly, 'there is something I must tell my husband.'

CHAPTER 7
SACRIFICE TO THE HEARTH GOD

Once he had her consent, Han-lao wasted no time in engaging the best doctor in Peking to supervise the unbinding of Ko-chin's feet.

'So today is the day,' Mrs Li said to the shrinking girl as she arrived to await the doctor's arrival in the apartment.

'Oh, honourable lady,' Ko-chin gasped, 'am I right to do this? I do not want great ugly feet and nor will my husband when he sees them!'

Mrs Li took Ko-chin's cold hands and chafed them between her own as she said gently, 'Child, forget the story that we women desire small feet in emulation of a girl some long-dead emperor loved. Remember only, as your husband does, that they are a cruel device to keep women imprisoned in their homes.'

'But the pain of the unbinding—' Ko-chin groaned.

'Command yourself, my nephew's wife,' Mrs Li told her with grave severity. 'This is your fate—accept it with dignity.' She raised her proud head. 'Ah, here they come; you may hold my hands, little one, and do not be so afraid. This doctor is a kind man.'

Han-lao would have stayed but his dismissal by Mrs Li, for all its courtesy, was very definite. He had to listen from behind the door-curtain, biting his lips, as Ko-chin had once done.

The servant who had brought hot water knelt before Ko-chin to take off the tiny laced shoes and the tight white stockings beneath. The doctor himself unwrapped the long bandages, then set Ko-chin's feet in the bowl of hot water to soak. Ko-chin tried to swallow down her panic but by the time the doctor piped to Mrs Li in his thin, high

55

voice, 'Honourable lady, the feet of this girl child were not well bound,' the merciful numbness was already beginning to wear off.

Behind the door-curtain, Han-lao shivered as the doctor went on, 'The big toe, of course, was left, but when the four small toes were drawn under to lie as flat as possible beneath the sole, their bones were broken too swiftly. Even in feet well bound, putting weight upon them when the soles have been forced back towards the heels is to bend them almost in half. In such a case as this, I fear in later age the feet would mortify and drop away. May the gods grant her a grateful heart for the fate that brought her to this house.'

'May the gods grant her strength too,' murmured Mrs Li. 'There is yet a long road in pain before her,' and Ko-chin licked her dry lips. Was there never an easy way for a woman?

When Ko-chin's feet had been dried, the doctor rebound them in fresh bandages, this first time only a very little less tightly than before. Then Han-lao was allowed to come in. He sank down beside her and took her hands in his. 'I know this is a bitter road for you, my wife,' he whispered, 'but it will be less bitter if you let me travel it beside you.'

Ko-chin raised blank eyes. Let him see her as she soon would be? Never. 'It is upon my own feet that I must walk, my lord,' she said evenly. 'Never fear but I shall do it. But when did a man ever walk beside a woman? It would not be fitting.'

And, as she turned her face away, Han-lao knew that she had retreated to some fastness in her own mind where he could not reach her. The barriers he had thought broken down between them were as high as ever. In sudden overwhelming fury at his helplessness, he left the room without another word: she had done as he wished but she would not let him help her through the ordeal, and for the wrong reasons. Oh, whatever had possessed him to take a wife? Women muddled everything, and now his life could never be simple and straightforward again.

But, as at every visit the doctor rebound Ko-chin's feet more loosely, and more blood forced its way into the long-disused channels of her broken feet, Han-lao found it impossible to distance himself from what was happening to her. He could gauge her pain by the fact that she no longer cared who heard her desperate sobbing, or her screams at the servant who stood guard to stop her tightening the bandages to re-numb her feet. At last he fought down his hurt pride and visited her room but she screamed at his touch too, when he bent to smooth the tangled hair away from her ravaged face.

In stunned grief he stumbled away to cry to his aunt, 'She's fifteen years old and she looks like an old woman—because of what I made her do! And she won't even let me try to comfort her!'

Mrs Li raised her delicate painted brows. 'How should she, my nephew? You must leave her some pride, even in this extremity. This is not for a husband to share.'

Han-lao groaned. If he couldn't make even his own wife understand how he longed to bridge the terrible gulf between men and women, how could he hope to explain to his aunt? It was the first time the proud son of the Li family had tasted failure and it was very bitter in his mouth.

Day after day, Ko-chin sat on her feet and rocked back and forth, the only way to ease the pain. She hardly noticed even when her sister was brought to her. Sung had been as good as his word—his friend, before returning to the south, had married Mo-ch'o, 'And I am to live here with you, sister, until my husband sends for me,' she whispered, pressing Ko-chin's wet cheek against her own.

But Ko-chin, eyes glazed, just rocked back and forth. The days seemed endless to Mo-ch'o before her sister smiled weakly at her for the first time, even began to take an interest in the messages of support sent by other reformers' wives. 'How strange,' Ko-chin muttered, 'I have never met these women, Mo-ch'o, but they write as if they really care about me—as though they too were my sisters! And I thought I was so alone . . . what has been happening these last weeks? Have you been listening as I did from behind the screen?'

Thin cheeks flushing, Mo-ch'o shook her head. 'Your husband has had no visitors, sister,' she murmured, 'and even if he had . . . '

She did not need to go on; what had they done to her, marrying her to a revolutionary, Ko-chin wondered bleakly. As for her own husband—it seemed an eternity since she had screamed at him to leave her room. Would he still be angry with her? When he returned that evening, even though he at once congratulated her on being able to stand again, she knew he was. There was no trace of the old questioning, shy, half smile that once had been just for her. She had put him at a distance and he had too much pride to trespass again. Yet now, seeing him look so tired and vulnerable, she longed to offer him the comfort she had not allowed him to give her.

But even as she moved uncertainly towards him, hot on the heels of the servant who announced him, Sung arrived. 'Han-lao—our leader—he is coming here, to Peking, to put before the Emperor a complete plan for reform!' he shouted.

'K'ang?' gasped Han-lao, eyes ablaze with excitement, and Ko-chin, knowing herself forgotten, limped quietly from the room; no mere wife could compete with the great K'ang.

And when Lan-kuei came for her first lesson since Ko-chin had unbound her feet she looked as sour as Ko-chin felt. 'Now there's to be a grand banquet to welcome K'ang to Peking,' the Manchu girl sniffed. 'Be sure we women will see nothing of our husbands until he is safely out of the city again. But I forget myself, Ko-chin—tell me, how are your poor feet?'

Lan-kuei's swift glance at the ugly new shoes poking out beneath the hem of Ko-chin's gown was very expressive and Ko-chin flushed, thinking bitterly, She's glad I've lost my lily feet. Now they make her own look less graceless! But aloud she only murmured, 'The worst is past, I thank you. Now, our lesson . . . '

'My forced labour, rather,' said Lan-kuei with an ugly twist to her lips. 'How I pity you, little Mo–ch'o, caught in the net with us!'

Mo–ch'o ducked her head, too overawed by this stately princess to answer, but Ko-chin knew she had no more relish for book learning than Lan-kuei. Between them, these two would suck her back into the past if they could. Ko-chin set her lips with new determination. She had not suffered so much to go backwards now; if need be she would drag these two with her into the future . . . with a bow towards the mutinous Lan-kuei she murmured, 'But the writing tools are set ready and use them I think we must, lady. Come, sit by me if you will . . . '

When the reformers' celebration dinner for K'ang was over, Ko-chin had been sure Han-lao would come to her to heal the rift between them, especially as the year was coming to its end and it would soon be time to send their Hearth God to report to Heaven his family's conduct. But the day before that ceremony, Ko-chin went in desperation to Mrs Li. Because, even though these days she hardly saw Han-lao, everything she did infuriated him. It was as though he hated her.

'Nothing I do is right, honourable lady,' she sobbed to Mrs Li. 'I know I would not let him help me when I unbound my feet, but do I deserve such punishment? I do not understand!'

Mo–ch'o, grateful that her own husband was so far away, clutched her sister's hand in silent sympathy but

Mrs Li only said with her usual tranquillity, 'Then learn to understand, my nephew's wife. Life has been too easy for your husband and, never having learnt to bend with the wind, he is bewildered now that he feels it turn against him. As his wife, it is for you to help him.'

'But how?' Ko-chin cried.

'By using the right he has given you to ask him what is wrong. Ask him, little one, about the great K'ang.'

Ko-chin stared, mouth ajar. What on earth could the great reform leader have to do with her humble life? And, as for asking Han-lao anything these days . . . 'What is it?' she snapped as a small hand tugged at her arm on the way back to her own apartment. Then, seeing the panic in Mo-ch'o's face, she controlled herself and managed to smile. 'Tell me, little sister,' she added gently.

Mo-ch'o drew a deep breath but couldn't find the words to tell this strong sister of her terror that the gods would punish the women of the household for Han-lao's careless contempt for all decent behaviour. Instead, she just muttered, 'Sister, tomorrow will be the twenty-third day of the twelfth month. I wondered—as your husband does not believe in the gods—whether he will allow us to make that day's proper sacrifices to the Hearth God?'

Ko-chin stared back at her. She hadn't thought of that. Of course Han-lao would not approve, but—she thought of how, even when her husband had come to her bed, she hadn't conceived a son. Was that the gods' punishment for her escape from old Chen? If so, they would be even angrier with her now, if she deliberately snubbed one of their number. 'I shall not ask him,' she declared. 'My husband has often told me that I must learn to decide things for myself and my decision is that we shall make the proper sacrifices tomorrow!'

Despite her bold words, Ko-chin's hands shook as she helped Mo-ch'o build a small wooden temple to put over the hearth. When Mo-ch'o had laid a picture of the god inside it, Ko-chin comforted herself by smearing his lips with honey: that way, he would only speak sweet words in Heaven and maybe the gods would let her be happy again.

Then Mo-ch'o lit the joss sticks and kindled the pine twig fire beneath the temple to send the god on his long journey. Clasping Ko-chin's hands, she breathed, 'There! Now he will bring back good luck for the New Year!'

They knelt a little longer beside the embers, each lost in her own thoughts. Ko-chin felt rather than heard the door-curtain drawn aside. She wheeled round to meet a look worse than any blow; then Han-lao turned on his heel, leaving the two stricken girls huddled together on the floor.

Ko-chin took no part in the household New Year celebrations and Mo-ch'o drifted through the rooms like a ghost, fearing what Ko-chin knew: that, having failed her husband, any day now she would be sent away. 'Then I shall kill myself,' Ko-chin whispered into the silence. When she heard hurried footsteps approaching, she took no notice, for who would be hurrying to find a rejected wife? The next moment, she was almost bowled over by Han-lao, who strode into the room and, dropping the firecrackers he carried, lifted her to her feet to press his face against her hair.

Ko-chin stood stunned, shocked to her soul at what she heard. Then she sobbed, 'Oh, husband, you must not debase yourself before me! I failed in my duty as a wife to obey what I knew would be your wishes!'

But he told her stormily, 'It is I, not you, who have failed! I promised never to ask you for blind obedience but, when I saw you behaving like a superstitious peasant, it seemed like another betrayal and I could not bear it.'

'Another betrayal, my lord?' she whispered, and felt his muscles tighten beneath his silken gown as he said harshly,

'K'ang! Oh, wife—' He swallowed hard, seeing again in his mind's eye the heavy, self-important face and shifting eyes of the leader he had once idolized. 'I brought you to Peking so sure he would lead us to victory with his plans to adapt Western ways to serve Chinese needs but now—Ko-chin, he is not the statesman we thought and, if he is rash enough to upset the Emperor's aunt, it may not be just the end of our reform movement—'

'But of us, too?' she whispered. 'Surely, though, it isn't too late to find another leader?'

He turned away, covering his face with his hands for a long moment. Then, stooping to gather up his spilled firecrackers, he muttered, 'Don't tempt the gods, wife. Another would-be leader is already on his way to Peking and when he arrives—well, I'll put it this way: beside T'an, our K'ang is as enslaved by the past as the Emperor's aunt!'

Ko-chin stared at him open-mouthed. 'Then this T'an is a revolutionary?' she breathed.

'He worships Western ways as much as he loathes our own,' Han-lao told her harshly. 'At least K'ang believes we should keep the best of our traditions and an Emperor at the head of government—T'an does not. He wants to set up Western legal and political institutions to run the country. Those who have fallen under his spell say he is like a meteor, scarring our dark sky with his light!'

'Oooh,' breathed Ko-chin. 'He sounds—extraordinary. But the Emperor would never listen to a revolutionary, would he?'

'Would he not!' said Han-lao grimly. 'T'an has a glamour that makes our poor K'ang look like a strutting chicken beside a soaring eagle. I think that when T'an tells the Emperor—who, remember, has always been fascinated by the West—that by trying to alter China gradually, and according to Chinese ways of thought, he is trying to bring back life to a corpse, he will listen. So, wife, we had better let off these firecrackers like everyone else, to make sure our Hearth God finds his way back home again—we may need his help before long!'

After the last firecrackers had sputtered away over the city, the silence was so uncanny that they both glanced up at the little square of sky above their courtyard. 'Oh, husband, who is taking the light?' Ko-chin cried.

Already the pale ovals of their upturned faces were fading in the thickening twilight. 'An eclipse,' Han-lao muttered, 'and on New Year's Day. But I didn't need that sign from Heaven to tell me we are on the brink of calamity. But, little wife, at least we will bear together whatever this new year may bring.'

'Whatever it may bring,' Ko-chin echoed as the shadow of the future swept across them. Then, 'The Reform Club meets at our apartment tonight, does it not, husband? This time I shall have company behind my screen, for my sister must be at least a little prepared for what her husband will expect of her!'

Even behind the safety of the screen, though, Mo-ch'o looked as if she had been lured to a den of dragons. She flinched as Han-lao's voice rang out with passionate bitterness, 'My friends, this leader of ours is like a child with a broken toy when he meets a setback! What use to us is a man who, when we can't arrange for him to meet the Emperor at once, groans, "It is all quite hopeless and I shall return to the mountains—the world is not ready for my message!"?'

There was a smouldering silence. Then the voice of an older man said wearily, 'Many of us feel as you do, Han-lao, but at least K'ang has a real strategy for ridding us of the foreigners over-running our land. Unlike our present ministers who can only parrot that Chinese intelligence really is superior to barbarian intelligence and that our present dilemma is only because we haven't yet got round to using it!'

'They've used all theirs up learning dead classics by heart to qualify them to be ministers in the first place,' Sung's deep voice said gloomily. 'So how can they hope to deal with invaders who have the science to understand how the real world works? At least K'ang is ready to learn from the West and, if only we can persuade him changes must be made as stealthily as silkworms nibbling mulberry leaves, in order to avoid upsetting the Emperor's aunt, we may yet—'

Sung broke off as a sharp voice cut across the servant's protest: 'Let me by, fool—I have news that cannot wait!'

Mo-ch'o clutched at Ko-chin, whimpering, 'Let us go, sister!' as, into the room's shocked silence, the voice shouted, 'Friends, our Emperor has come to his senses at last—demands to know why his ministers cannot stop the foreign devils pillaging our land and—'

'Will you not sit down, Ting-i?' Han-lao's voice, icy in its restraint, cut through the tirade. 'My servant will fetch you fresh tea.'

'Drink tea? When the Emperor has summoned K'ang to his presence?' rasped the hateful voice. 'What kind of reformer are you, Han-lao? Even your wife still hides behind a screen! Isn't it time we reformers saw this over-modest creature?' And he struck the screen with the flat of his hand, so that it fell back against the cowering girls behind.

'What would you know of modest women, Ting-i?' spat Han-lao. 'Your mind is an undrained sewer and the stink of it pollutes everything around you!'

A deathly hush fell, broken only by Mo-ch'o's sobs. For two young men to strip away one another's face so brutally was beyond the bounds of all civilized behaviour! What had brought things to this pass between them, Ko-chin wondered in frozen terror. Could Sung have meant Ting-i when he had spoken of old Chen's son vowing vengeance on Han-lao? Thank Heaven she could hear men moving—they would not stay for their meeting now. Someone, with carefully averted face, was lifting the screen, helping her to her feet.

No hope now, after such a scene, that this would be the night when the gods relented and let them make a son, Ko-chin thought drearily, and Han-lao bit his lip as he caught her sad glance. He had punished her enough recently for things that were not her fault and so, much as he would have preferred to be alone, he went to her room. When he saw how her eyes lit up, he knew he had done the right thing for himself as well as her.

'Oh, wife,' he blurted, 'you see now the kind of pressures some of us are putting on K'ang! When we should be treading as if we walked on eggshells, fanatics like Ting-i are pushing for immediate action—they don't seem able to understand that, if she sees any threat to her own or her allies' positions, the Emperor's aunt will crush him with as little pity as she would a beetle.'

'Oh, I am so afraid of that Ting-i,' Ko-chin whispered, 'but, my husband, you must remember that even the Emperor's aunt cannot stop the world from changing if the time is ripe. However it comes about, such huge change must be painful for us all—but remember too how afraid I was to unbind my feet, and how glad I am now that I did!'

Han-lao stared at her for a long moment, then covered his face with his hands.

CHAPTER 8
SMASHING RICE BOWLS

Thank Heaven that the long scorching summer that had followed the unbinding of her feet was almost over, thought Ko-chin, pausing for a few moments to savour the first autumn chill in her little courtyard. Maybe now some sanity would return to Peking and the feverish pace of reform slow down enough to let them breathe again. She no longer asked herself if such upheaval was worth it, though, not now that she understood how urgent was the need to stop the foreigners carving up China between them like a great juicy melon.

'If only our ancestors had agreed to trade with the Westerners, instead of treating them as if they were below contempt and slamming our door in their faces,' she said softly to her peonies, 'would things have been any different for us now? Or are barbarians so greedy that they would have swallowed us alive even sooner?' She sighed and went indoors: Lan-kuei would soon be here for her lesson—but Han-lao arrived before the Manchu girl.

'There's to be an emergency Reform Club meeting here,' he told her abruptly, 'warn the servant to prepare tea.'

Ko-chin, stomach flipping nervously, ran herself to fetch tea bowls. What now? Had the Emperor's aunt moved against them at last? Ko-chin almost wished she had; at least it would break this awful tension of waiting for the reaction that must come from the Palace of Kindly and Tranquil Old Age, where the Emperor's aunt was besieged by infuriated ministers with news of the Emperor's latest decrees. Not, from a reformer's point of view, that the decrees were bad ones: there were just too many too soon . . . once K'ang had been granted the incredibly rare privilege of contacting the Emperor directly, he had proved as greedy as any barbarian, hurtling China into the future with never a thought for those whose rice bowls his reforms were smashing, as age-old positions, rights and incomes were summarily abolished. Soon the backlash must come—was it to be today?

Breathing hard, she stopped outside Mo-ch'o's room. It was high time her little sister came to a meeting: as well as being her duty to her husband, it would prepare her for what might come . . . too frightened herself to be gentle, Ko-chin hustled Mo-ch'o to the room where already Reform Club members were gathering. Mo-ch'o wished she was dead: eyes fixed on the floor, she stumbled to the seat beside Lan-kuei, who felt her shaking and gently took her hand. Poor little Mo-ch'o! Had Ko-chin forgotten how hard it was to break old taboos? At least, in the early days, *she* had been allowed the protection of a screen . . . but, thought Lan-kuei bitterly, since the releasing of Ko-chin's feet from their crippling bonds, she had become so self-possessed and confident that she could speak her mind before anyone. Beside her, these days, the Manchu princess felt heavy, lumpish—stupid! It was all the fault of these hateful 'reforms'. Before, Sung would never have set eyes on his friend's wife; he might have gone to flower girls but they were no threat to a wife's position. But now—who knew where such improper freedom between the sexes might end? Lan-kuei shuddered. Even worse would be if the Emperor's aunt found out where one of her own ladies-in-waiting was at this very minute.

'I hate them all,' she glowered, 'all except poor little Mo-ch'o. She is as trapped as I am in this idiot conspiracy! I wonder what we're waiting for now—and where is my husband?'

She glanced furtively round the room. The other visitors were sipping their tea quietly enough but tension fizzed in the air. At last one of them muttered, 'Where is Sung? He must know by now whether we've been able to keep our young meteor T'an from meeting the Emperor!'

So that was it! Ko-chin flushed hotly, remembering how Han-lao's descriptions of this young firebrand after his arrival in Peking had so fired her imagination that she had asked to meet him herself. 'Certainly not,' Han-lao had snapped. 'He is not a suitable person for a young woman to meet.' Then, when she had persisted, 'Really, wife, once you would agree to meet no one, now you pester to see every other young man who comes to Peking!'

Ko-chin had snapped back, 'If that is a fault in me, my husband, you encouraged it!' That was the first time she had ever answered him back. Any other husband would have beaten her for it . . .

Ko-chin jumped as the door-curtain swished aside to reveal Sung's tall figure. He gazed down at the circle of pale faces raised towards him, his lips not quite steady: they were so young, these men and girls, to have pitted their wits against the might of a crusted empire. What would happen to them now? He swallowed before saying huskily, 'I have to tell you T'an answered the Emperor's summons this morning, and what sanity was left to our movement has been abandoned. Not only has the Emperor's aunt now been told of K'ang's slanders against her—such as, she murdered her son's wife, sleeps with eunuchs, ordered the Emperor's feet branded with red-hot irons—but, in a day or two, she will have proof that the Emperor is deliberately toppling his dynasty's own government. Then she will bring in the army. I urge those of you who can leave Peking to do so at once.' He turned to Lan-kuei, 'Wife, we must return to the Forbidden City to make sure our own loyalty to the government is not put in doubt.'

Lan-kuei scuttled to his side with not so much as a glance at Ko-chin. She felt no sense of betrayal. She had never wanted to be here in the first place and as Manchus there was no need for herself or Sung to share whatever fate awaited these Chinese. She hurried towards the Gate of Peaceful Escape, heart singing: even her husband must have the sense to shake loose before it was too late.

It never occurred to Ko-chin that Han-lao would leave Peking, even when a frantic message told them that one of the great armies loyal to the Emperor's aunt had been stationed outside the city's gates, and she was not surprised that Sung's arguments fell on deaf ears. 'I can only protect you and your family so far, Han-lao,' he raged two days after the Emperor had seen T'an. 'Not content with toppling whole government bureaux at a stroke, today the Emperor intends to dismiss his aunt's favourite minister. After that, I have it on the best authority his aunt will smash him once and for all.'

Ko-chin drew closer to Han-lao, although in front of Sung she would not take the hand he stretched towards her. 'Lord,' she said softly, before Han-lao could speak— tempers in Peking these days caught fire as swiftly as summer-dried grass—'My husband hears you but—'

Their servant's abrupt arrival, spluttering, 'Master, I told him he could not enter!' caught her in mid-sentence. Ting-i pushed the old man aside. Behind him, a taller shadow blocked the light. Ko-chin had her wish—T'an had come.

Ting-i's laugh was shrill, taunting: 'I have brought our new leader to see how the women of Peking are joining in our fight,' he hissed, 'for such beauty should not go unremarked, unrewarded!'

But Ting-i's wildness seemed a shadowy thing beside the aura of raw brilliance that emanated from his silent companion. Ko-chin felt that T'an's look physically scorched her before Han-lao moved to block her from his gaze. She only heard the impact of her husband's hand across Ting-i's face, then Ting-i's snarl, 'That insult shall be avenged in blood, Manchu-lover and stealer of women!'

Ko-chin threw her arms around Han-lao to hold him back but their uninvited guests had gone. T'an had said nothing; the meteor's course across the Chinese sky was almost run.

Tears streamed down Ko-chin's face. That Han-lao should have so demeaned himself as to strike someone because of her! It was all her fault for being there—and what would Ting-i do in revenge? Oblivious of Sung, she began to sob in earnest. Could a woman never do anything right? Oh, if only the gods had granted her a son she would not have been here this afternoon and this would never have happened.

Leaving Mo-ch'o to comfort her, Han-lao flung out of the apartment to hear the latest teahouse news—news that left him feeling blacker than ever. But later, when Ko-chin had seen him settled with fresh tea, then quietly edged towards the door, he muttered, 'Stay and talk to me, wife. I do not wish to be alone.'

'You look so tired,' she whispered, sinking down beside him.

'But not tired of you,' he told her with the small half smile she loved. 'Oh, Ko-chin, to see you insulted as I did this morning—not even all reformers are to be trusted!' She laid her cheek against the cool silk of his gown and his hand slipped to caress her hair. 'Perhaps, after all, there are good reasons behind some of the old ways . . . '

Ko-chin jerked her head away from his hand. 'But you cannot mean that, lord,' she gasped. 'You have opened the world to me! What is one insult compared to a lifetime spent half asleep?' But he did not answer and she knew a dangerous seed had been sown in his mind that day. 'Come to bed, my husband,' she whispered.

'Not yet, little wife,' he said ruefully. 'I am playing truant from tonight's meeting to decide what those left of us should do and Sung will be calling later to let me know. Wait with me, since he at least can be trusted not to sully your honour.'

He was smiling but Ko-chin felt another small cold qualm, knowing Han-lao would never be quite so certain or trusting again—and changes in him meant change for her. And when she saw the savagery in Sung's face, she wished she had not waited, although when she crept towards the door he exclaimed, voice as gentle as it could ever be, 'Forgive me, my friend's wife, I did not see you there. Do not go, I need both of you to calm me after tonight's display of idiocy. No tea, I thank you, I have already drunk too much wine.'

Then, spitting his words like barbarian bullets, Sung described the last reformers' meeting to them. 'K'ang like a smoky old lamp, our meteor T'an quenched—spineless defeat on every side, blaming all this fiasco on the Emperor's aunt.'

'Everything is her fault according to K'ang these days,' snapped Han-lao. 'But would things have been any different if she had never been born?'

Ko-chin, as always when she listened to their talk, had forgotten everything else, even their own danger. 'But surely,' she put in eagerly, 'if the land brings forth rotten fruit, it is the land, not the fruit, at fault?'

Sung smiled at her. 'So you are saying our Emperor's aunt has no choice but to be the old rotten that she is! I fear you are right, my friend's wife, and probably that wretched T'an is too when he says the only way forward is to turn the present system upside down, but I wish he had let us at least try less radical solutions first.'

Ko-chin frowned. 'But, my husband's friend, our system is founded upon the teachings of Confucius who said we must always copy the past and never let anything new happen. So, if we are ever to change really, then we must exchange Confucius first!'

She heard Han-lao swallow. Then Sung said wryly, 'Perhaps you should have allowed your wife to talk with our revolutionary T'an after all, my friend!' Han-lao shook his head dazedly as Sung addressed Ko-chin directly: 'My friend's wife, tell me, have you yet heard us speak of Dr Sun Yat-sen, the leader of the revolutionary movement in the south to which your sister's husband belongs?'

Shyly she nodded and, although no doubt he only teased, Han-lao glanced sharply at his friend as he suggested, 'Maybe, at heart, you are not a reformer at all, Ko-chin, but a revolutionary?'

Ko-chin's mouth fell open. 'Can that be?' she gasped, so comically staggered that a great wave of laughter shook Han-lao as well as Sung. Cheeks flushed, Ko-chin ducked her head but she tingled all over as though she had drunk a deep draught of wine. Was that what Han-lao, without meaning to, had taught her to be? Would he be angry? She was so muddled—where would all this thinking end? Her reeling thoughts scattered as Sung, suddenly sober again, blurted, 'I did not know women could be—if only my own wife . . . ' He stopped, face dark with sudden pain. Then, 'I must go now. Goodnight, my friends.'

When the sound of his boots had died away, Han-lao said wonderingly, 'I did not know women could be like you, either.'

'If I am at all different from others of my sex,' Ko-chin told him softly, 'it is you who made me so. But, perhaps, given the chance, all of us . . . '

'Maybe so,' Han-lao muttered, 'but will they ever get the chance now, or will that old woman in the Forbidden City make sure that no one ever dares to try to change anything again?'

Ko-chin rose to her feet. 'She will not live forever, husband,' she said steadily, 'nor will the foreigners leave our gates. Be sure our children will know a different world, whatever the price we pay for it.'

CHAPTER 9

THE VERMILION PENCIL

In so much turmoil, no one had time for the unimportant little sister, Mo-ch'o, hovering terror-stricken on the edge of events. But when, at the Hour of the Cock when at last light was creeping over the sky, she heard Han-lao return from an emergency meeting, she crept to find at least the comfort of other human beings. But Ko-chin, hurrying with hot rice gruel for Han-lao, pushed her aside—she moved so fast these days—and Mo-ch'o felt the door-curtain fall softly back against her face, shutting her out. Her face like a frosted peony petal amid the shadows, she heard Han-lao saying, 'So many hopes, wife—all wrecked through sheer stupidity! No, I cannot eat. There have been messages from the Emperor—his aunt will use armed force if he doesn't end all the reforms at once, and K'ang will be executed if he ever comes near the Emperor again! And oh, Ko-chin—' Han-lao's voice broke, '—he begs us to find a way to save him!'

Tears washed Mo-ch'o's face as she heard Ko-chin choke, 'We must do something—'

'Oh, we are,' Han-lao interrupted savagely. 'A plan so lunatic that the mind boggles! T'an has gone to the only army general on our side to tell him that his superior officer—who just happens to be a favourite of the Emperor's aunt and in command of an army of 100,000 men!—is plotting to dethrone and murder the Emperor.'

'But is that true?' Mo-ch'o heard Ko-chin's terrified whisper.

'Not that I know of,' Han-lao snarled. 'But even if it was, we would need written proof. To ask any soldier to murder his superior officer and take over the capital—oh, yes, that is what T'an has gone to ask him, wife!—is more than folly: it's suicide.'

Mo-ch'o clasped her arms around her thin body. How would Han-lao treat the women of his household when his last dream for a new future was dead? She heard her own dread echo in Ko-chin's voice: 'But surely the Emperor's letters are enough proof that he's in terrible danger?'

'Those letters were written in black ink. It is only decrees written in the Vermilion Pencil that every man must obey or die. Our little general can make up his own mind who it would be in his best interests to support; and he's not a stupid man. Within a few hours the Emperor's aunt will have the last ammunition she needs to finish us; proof positive that Reform Club members have tried to persuade one of her soldiers to murder her favourite general and imprison her Imperial Self.'

'Then there is no hope . . . '

'None.'

Mo-ch'o hobbled away; Ko-chin would have no time to listen to a little sister's problems today. In her own room, hand over her eyes, Mo-ch'o sat down before her mirror. Could it be true, what she had heard those servants whispering yesterday? Not just that she was so ugly that her husband must hate her, but that her body was too frail ever to bear sons? Because if it was . . . Mo-ch'o put her other hand across her face. Beauty—how she had longed for it. The eyebrows like narrow willow leaves; the mouth a tiny ripe cherry set in the oval face of classic beauty. Eyes like black pearls and little ears close to the head, so that rings of jade and gold would cling close. Mo-ch'o dropped her hands and looked in the mirror. Not one thing right, and dull skin, scant hair, darkened teeth as well. Her tiny body spoke for itself.

The servants were right. Should her husband ever return, he would reject her—doubtless already had. Which meant that she would be as homeless in death as in life, for her spirit, denied a place in her husband's home, could not even return to her own family's home. And soon they were all going to die—silently, fighting down her sobs in case anyone should hear, Mo-ch'o wept in an agony of despair.

Outside in the city, the silence was profound, its sole pulse beating behind the coloured walls of the Forbidden City. Only one message came to the House of Li: Sung's servant stuttering, 'The Emperor's aunt knows everything and eunuchs loyal to our Emperor have been strangled—his Imperial Self imprisoned! K'ang has fled and my master commands you to stay within doors until we know where the Imperial lightning will strike next!'

For the first time that day, Mo-ch'o spoke then: 'Will the Emperor's aunt be sending her soldiers to this house, my sister?' she cried wildly. 'Shall we be strangled, too?'

Ko-chin clasped the girl tightly in her arms but neither she nor Han-lao told her what she knew already: that now no house harbouring a reformer was safe. After a moment, Mo-ch'o gently released herself and left Ko-chin alone with her husband.

Like hammer blows every day now the news came flying on wildfire wings, until even Mo-ch'o's mind was numbed: the Emperor had handed over the reins of government to his aunt—had signed death warrants—the Pearl Concubine, begging to share his imprisonment, had been condemned to the Palace of Forgotten Concubines, to live on a beggar's diet of coarsest rice and cabbage; while he mouldered amid the beauty of the Ocean Terrace, cut off from the world by a rosy lake of late-blooming lotus lilies, the Pearl's beauty would decay in loneliness.

'But it was her own fault,' Mo-ch'o muttered feverishly to herself, crouched by the goldfish pond in their little Court of the Peonies. 'She chose her danger!'

Indoors, they were talking again. How she loathed the sound of voices now! Where had all their talk got them? So six reformers had been executed, the meteor T'an among them: why was her sister's husband so excited about T'an's last words? Quoting them, his voice had echoed through the courtyard where she had hoped to find some peace: '"I am willing to shed my blood to save my country—but know that for each one of us who dies today, a thousand will rise up to carry on our work of reform! We are not defeated."'

Fool, with his empty words! They were all prisoners of one another. Eyes closed, Mo-ch'o laid her hands on the cool flagstones around the pool. Above, the cool autumn sunlight which she had watched glancing from the sliding forms of the goldfish had gone, and the light was fading. Soon, the courtyard's peonies would shrivel in the bitter cold of another Peking winter . . . but the life of this great family house would go on. Already, as the Hour of the Dog drew near, the servants were lighting the first lamps of evening, even though that meteor T'an was dead. Slowly, as lights shone softly from the house, somewhere a harp's strings rippled, mothers' voices called in their children, and Mo-ch'o suddenly longed for the homely indoor odours of cowfat candles and incense, sweetmeats and savoury food being prepared in the kitchens.

Before she passed inside, though, Mo-ch'o glanced up at the square of sky above the courtyard. 'All under Heaven'—that was what they said. 'Oh, Kuan-yin, Goddess of Mercy, show me my way,' she breathed. 'Before I die, let me find a way to command myself!' And then, for the first time in many weeks, she smiled. She was as wild in dreams as Ko-chin, to ask such an impossible freedom!

In her room, though, she changed her grey gown for one of blue, the colour that uplifted the spirit and sent it wandering, and, when she heard Ko-chin cry out, she went to her without hesitation, even though she knew the terrible Prince Sung was there.

'Oh, my husband, you must listen to our friend,' Ko-chin was wailing. She whirled round when Mo-ch'o slipped into the room. 'Oh, sister, our friend has told us how narrowly my husband has escaped execution but he has gone mad!'

Sung looked enormous, towering over them, face black with anger, but Han-lao snarled, 'You dared to say I was a luke-warm reformer—a young fool badly influenced!'

'I did,' Sung ground back. 'Futile heroics aren't my style, if they are yours. Accept that your role for the next few months is to look grateful that your head is still on your shoulders and learn how to keep it that way.'

Clutching Mo-ch'o's arm, Ko-chin gabbled, 'How can we ever thank you, our friend, for thinking so quickly to save my husband! We will take your advice, of course.'

But there was no 'of course' about it. Ko-chin looked in despair at Han-lao's slumped figure after Sung had gone. How could she convince him it was worth staying alive, rather than giving the Reform Movement another martyr for the history books? Then, against her ear, Mo-ch'o's voice whispered, 'Forget our country's needs for now, sister. Remind your husband of his first duty—to keep open the bridge between past and future by making sons.'

Of course! Even before Mo-ch'o had slipped away, Ko-chin's brain had snapped out of bemused misery into action. With an incisiveness that jerked Han-lao, from sheer surprise, out of his nightmare thoughts, she said, 'My husband, I know you care little for the duties you owe your parents and your ancestors, so I will not beg you to preserve your life for their sakes. But think of this, if you refuse to take our friend's advice, you risk not only your own life but the lives of your future sons.'

'But—' Han-lao began—

'I know that you say you want no sons,' Ko-chin cut in, still in that extraordinary new voice, 'but who will carry on the fight to reform our land, when we are gone, if all the best reformers deliberately throw away their lives at the first setback? That's just what our enemies want us to do!'

He frowned and she held her breath. She could think of no other argument which might persuade him; and, even if he accepted it, if she didn't provide him with the promise of a son in the very near future, for how long would he be able to endure the inaction, the boredom of a confined life? Men knew nothing of the strategies of survival women were forced to learn from childhood . . . Once Ko-chin was sure that, for the moment at least, she had won, she fled to Mrs Li.

'Oh, my husband's aunt,' she cried, 'advise me, I beg you! I am so afraid that I am barren!'

At first, Mrs Li had seemed as far away in her mind as Han-lao had been earlier, but seeing Ko-chin's frantic face, with a visible effort she straightened her slender shoulders and smiled. This young wife's body was as tautly held as an archer's bowstring but her eyes were lustrous, she moved with easy grace: her seeming fragility, Mrs Li thought, was surely only skin deep . . . Aloud she murmured, 'I think not, little one. Everything has been so new, so strange for you, it is more likely that your body dares not relax to let Nature take her course. Once you have learnt tranquillity of mind, then your body will do as it should.'

'But my life is not tranquil—so how can I be?' protested Ko-chin indignantly.

'By learning, as every woman must, to go with your fate,' Mrs Li told her, already turning away.

But Ko-chin, made bold by desperation, caught at her sleeve: 'But my fate has been to learn how to become abnormal, honourable lady! Can it—oh, can it really be possible for a woman allowed to talk, and to think for herself as I am allowed to do, to conceive like a normal woman?'

Her deepest fear spoken aloud at last, Ko-chin collapsed in tears. Through blurred eyes, she saw the pale profile of this lady of the house as coldly unmoved as carved ivory. 'I beg your pardon, my husband's aunt,' she choked. 'I should not speak so to you. I will return to my apartment—'

But this time it was Mrs Li who stretched out a hand. A single tear slid down her cheek. 'Do not think I do not understand how hard it is to deal with so different a life, Ko-chin,' she said softly. 'Today my own youngest brother died by the executioner's sword for the Reform Movement. But we women must send our menfolk out whole into the struggle, though it drains our hearts' blood. Let each new ordeal teach you fortitude, little one, because you will need all the strength you can find in the years ahead of us. Today's bloodletting has been only the prologue.'

The silvery light filtered through the mother-of-pearl window lattices and the apple-green of Ko-chin's gown glowed richly beside the pale folds of the older woman's gown; they stood side by side, as still as painted figures from the past, as their unfettered minds fretted at the unknown future.

It was Ko-chin who broke the silence at last, murmuring, 'When I unbound my feet, my husband told me that the longest journey begins with the first step. But I do not think that he understands, as I do now, that such a journey as we reformers wish to make may take more than one lifetime. Perhaps it is my turn to teach him now—but even as a new woman I cannot do that without sons.'

Mrs Li smiled at her painfully. This wife of her nephew was learning but—'Say you have not a son but a daughter, little one?' she asked gently.

Ko-chin did not answer. Their new world was still only a dream for the future; meanwhile, she had to live as best she could in the old. If Han-lao was selfish enough to martyr himself, she would be left as a 'bird with one wing'—a widow, who would be expected to spend the rest of a chaste life in mourning for him. Without his sons to console her and give her status in his mother's house, she would have nothing left to live for at all. Even to a new woman, a daughter was of no use.

CHAPTER 10

EATING TADPOLES

The northern winter had been long and bitter—in more ways than one, thought Ko-chin, prodding at the rotting ice on their little goldfish pool. But in the world outside, spring was stirring and no more of the Emperor's servants need lose their heads for smuggling him warmer clothing. Poor, poor man; Ko-chin wiped her eyes, remembering how even his one attempt at escape had failed because he had not had the heart to abandon his servants to torture and death. Han-lao, in the ugly, frozen anger that possessed him these days, had said he despised him for that, but Ko-chin did not. It had been out of compassion that Han-lao had married her: what kind of new world could they build if they threw pity for pain overboard in the making of it? But these days he didn't seem to care who he hurt. A fine way for a would-be reformer to behave! And as for his promise that they would make a son, he had not been near her bed for weeks.

Sullenly, Ko-chin turned her back on the fleeting sunshine and went indoors again. Soon farmers would be bringing into the city the fresh young greens, radishes, garlic, turnips, onions, that would renew the blood after winter's heavy diet. But what was the point of renewing *her* blood, when already it surged through her body, making her want to scream with restlessness? At least bound feet, slowing the circulation, hindering movement, had made forever being within walls bearable! Ko-chin glared at the tall vase picturing docile women with empty smiles—was that one journey to Peking, that one tantalizing glimpse of the city, to last her the rest of her life? Before she even knew what she meant to do, she darted across the room, seized the vase, and hurled it against the tiled floor!

Servants came running. 'Go!' she shouted. They went. A few moments later, Mo-ch'o's face peeped round the curtain and Ko-chin, her frayed nerves soothed by that tremendous smash, began to laugh. 'It's all right, little sister,' she choked, propping herself against a chair, 'I haven't gone mad—not quite!'

Mo-ch'o knelt to gather up the pieces, then looked up at Ko-chin and smiled. 'Do you feel better now?' she asked.

'I do! But if my husband doesn't let me use these new feet of mine outside this house I may not for long,' Ko-chin told her. 'But, little sister, why are you so pretty today?'

Mo-ch'o ducked her head. 'I am to visit the Buddhist temple with your husband's aunt,' she said softly.

'Oh! Is it a festival day? Well, you must not keep her waiting,' said Ko-chin rather blankly. 'I will clear up those pieces.'

Mo-ch'o, with something of her own to do! Now Ko-chin thought about it, her little sister had been different these last weeks—less jumpy, less shadowy. And often Ko-chin had found her praying . . . what had changed her? Deep in thought, Ko-chin knocked to the floor a pile of handbills she hadn't noticed before. Crossly she dropped to her knees again to gather them up, then paused as their lurid colours caught her eye. What were these? Han-lao must have brought them back last night. They were hateful! A crucified pig—she pored over the smudged characters: something to do with that foreign god . . . another one with a slogan, 'Overthrow the Dynasty and expel the barbarian!'

When Han-lao came in she was still on her knees, bent in horrid fascination over the characters which ranted vitriolic loathing for Manchus and foreign devils alike. 'Leave those alone,' he snapped, snatching them up.

She didn't move. 'But do the people believe what these say?' she whispered.

'Since the Boxers are telling them exactly what they want to hear, many do,' Han-lao said curtly. He crumpled a bundle of them between his hands, eyes blank as he stared at the wall. He hadn't even noticed the missing vase.

'Boxers?' faltered Ko-chin.

'Gangs of youths who claim that the old religious rite of shadow boxing has given them magical protection against all weapons, even western bullets.'

'But can that be true?' Ko-chin cried.

Han-lao shrugged. 'That's beside the point. It's what the people believe that's important, and they'll believe anyone who promises to rid them of an Emperor who can't stop foreign devils ruining their livelihoods. Think of all those railway lines other countries have insisted on building here, putting our own chairbearers, camelmen, carters, muleteers out of work—and that's only one example. So the people are cheering the Boxers every inch of their way to Peking. They're close enough now for Sung and I to go ourselves to one of their demonstrations tomorrow.'

Ko-chin scrambled to her feet panting, 'And I—I will come too, husband! I beg you—'

He stared at her in just the same way that the servants had stared when she had broken the vase. Then, dropping his eyes, he muttered, 'That's impossible—you know it is. It will be a long journey on rough roads and the demonstration itself will be—'

'Dangerous?' she cried. 'But why did I unbind my feet if I am always to be protected? What use was it to throw away all my pretty shoes to wear these great things if I'm never to go anywhere in them?'

He took her hands gently but she was in no mood to be soothed. She pulled away, sobbing, 'You'd rather I worried myself half to death alone here, knowing how light you hold your life! And you will be with the Prince

Sung, who would never sink to disguise himself just for a Manchu-hating rabble!'

'But I promise, wife, I will take every care both for myself and for him—'

'But I want to share something with you, so I can understand better when you are unhappy,' Ko-chin wailed.

'Wife—' There was an edge to Han-lao's voice now that told her better than his words that she was beaten, '—you say you want to be a mother: to do that, you must be tranquil—'

Oh, that word again! Ko-chin dropped her hands from her face and glared up at him. 'I would be more tranquil if I could use my body as well as my mind,' she snapped. 'Since my feet were unbound, husband, I feel so much better—the blood courses through my veins, I want to walk, run!'

He turned to the door. Pulling the curtain aside, he said so quietly she could hardly hear him, 'But it is such a world out there. The old ways are cruel, but I'm beginning to think I've been even crueller, giving you false hopes of freedom.' And the curtain swung silently back behind him.

Tranquillity. How did you find it? Learn it, then you will conceive, Mrs Li had told her. But how, with one dreadful thing after another to torture her mind? And even if she did conceive, how could a child born to a nerve-racked mother have a fortunate life?

Oddly enough, it was Mo-ch'o who cheered her up. Lan-kuei was to come to them the day Han-lao and Sung went to the Boxer meeting: 'Oh, sister,' Mo-ch'o said excitedly, 'do you think your friend the Princess will tell us about Her Majesty's tea-party for the foreign ladies when she comes?'

'Maybe,' said Ko-chin, heart lightening to see at least her sister happier, 'although we must not bother her with too many questions; always remember that she only comes here because her husband makes her.'

When Lan-kuei did arrive, she looked so regal in her court robes of scarlet and gold, glittering with gems, that she took both their breaths away for a moment. Then Ko-chin breathed, 'How gorgeous you look, our friend! But so tired—'

Lan-kuei smiled wearily. 'Such gowns are heavy to wear when you have to stand for five hours at a time. I thought I would drop long before Her Majesty's guests departed.' Then, as the steaming tea Ko-chin brought revived her, angry blood surged into her face, prickling the heavy overlay of paint unbearably. Both Ko-chin and Mo-ch'o jumped as her pent-up anger suddenly exploded into words: 'Oh, how I wish my husband had not made me learn so much English! The things those so-called foreign "ladies" said about us, not caring that we might understand what they were saying—mocking us—discussing how much our gowns must have cost—one of them even fingered the material of mine, just as if there was no one inside it!' Lan-kuei tugged at the silken folds furiously. 'I shall never wear this again!'

'But surely Her Majesty protested,' cried Ko-chin.

'Not her.' Lan-kuei scowled. 'She kept saying to them, "Western or Eastern, we are all one family", even though she knows how the Boxers are working the people up to murder every foreign devil in the country!'

'And your Manchu dynasty too,' Ko-chin pointed out gently.

Lan-kuei laughed harshly. 'Oh, that won't last! The Emperor's aunt much likes what her advisers tell her of the Boxers' plans for casting out the foreign devils—and, anyway, if the Boxers have won the people's hearts, it would be unsafe to deny them . . . '

'For your Manchu dynasty maybe,' said Ko-chin angrily, 'but for China—'

At once Lan-kuei's face changed. How dare a mere Chinese criticize her people! 'Oh, Boxers love you reformers no more than barbarians. *They* don't want to learn from countries which have deliberately poisoned our people with opium for huge profits, while prating about their "god of love"!'

The two girls glared at one another and Mo-ch'o stood up. 'Ladies,' she said quietly, 'why quarrel? For what will be will be. All that is within our scope for change is in learning how to be kinder to one another.'

Ko-chin flushed with shame. To be chided by her little sister like that! Lan-kuei, though, crumpled in her seat. 'But what good is that, if things already suit our husbands very well as they are? Whatever they say, they don't want any real changes in their own homes. Ko-chin was made to unbind her feet, but has she ever been allowed to use them?' And she began to cry.

Swiftly Ko-chin put her arms around her and, while Mo-ch'o ran for hot towels, whispered, 'Will you not tell me why you are so unhappy, my friend?'

'Because my husband will not allow me to have a son!' she sobbed, beyond pride now. 'That is well enough now, while I am young, but later, if I have no sons to hold him . . . '

While Mo-ch'o gingerly wiped Lan-kuei's blotched face, Ko-chin said firmly, 'Dear friend, we all know that only Heaven has the power to decide when you shall have a child—not your husband!'

'That's what you think,' choked Lan-kuei. 'But he sent for an old woman to teach me what women past their fortieth year do to stop having children. Oh, Ko-chin, she made me swallow fourteen live tadpoles at the right time of the month, and ten more the next day, so that I won't be able to conceive for five whole years!'

Ko-chin gasped, 'Even one live tadpole would make me sick.'

Lan-kuei managed a watery smile. 'But you have not eaten that one, have you?'

Before Ko-chin could answer, the door curtain swayed in a sudden draught and, ecstatic with relief, she cried, 'Our husbands are back! I must make fresh tea for them!'

Nobody drank that tea, though. The sight of Sung with a blood-stained bandage around his head shattered what was left of Lan-kuei's endurance. She sat smouldering as Han-lao, trying to explain, told more than he had meant to tell of what they had seen. Boxers foaming at the mouth, whirling great swords around their heads, screaming that they were great men come back from the past to cleanse the land of foreign devils and those Chinese who, by eating the foreign religion, had become 'secondary devils' . . . then the great burning alive of secondary devils that had been the climax of the demonstration . . .

'And the peasants loved every minute of it,' said Sung harshly. 'Especially when one of them came at me with a sword! But you needn't look so distressed, wife—once they are sure of our government's support, they will concentrate on killing foreigners rather than Manchus.'

With a choking sound Lan-kuei rose to her feet. Tall in her gold and scarlet, she stood silent for a moment, collecting herself, then she said with forced calm, 'Take me home, husband, where you may humiliate me in private.'

Ko-chin had never seen Sung look ashamed before. When they had gone she breathed, 'Poor Lan-kuei. He has broken the pattern of her life and given her nothing in return. I beg you, my husband, do not do the same to me.'

For a moment, Han-lao did not understand her. Then he opened his arms to her—even though, with his head full of hideous images of death, he could not imagine creating new life.

CHAPTER 11
FOREIGN DEVIL

'The various powers cast upon us looks of tiger-like voracity. Let us not think of making peace!' That was what the Emperor's aunt was saying, even as the Boxers promised, 'Eight million spirit soldiers will descend from Heaven to help us sweep our Empire clean of barbarians!'

But Ko-chin didn't worry about that now: the gods could not be so cruel as to allow a war when, at long, long last, she was almost sure she had happiness within her. The summer season of luscious yellow-fleshed sweet melons she loved was nearly over; soon, she must tell Han-lao that, by next spring, they would have their first son . . . then there would be something better to talk about than Boxers!

But, in the meantime, she frowned as Lan-kuei asked, 'Is it really true, what the Boxers are saying, that if a man drinks a glass of tea offered by a foreign godman, his brains will burst out of his skull? Or that the Christians are poisoning all the wells?'

'Plenty of poor fools believe it is,' said Sung scornfully, 'even to the extent of pouring away well water to drain off the poison. But use your brains, wife: foreigners want us to buy their goods and we can't do that if we're dead!'

Ko-chin, knowing that beneath her heavy make-up Lan-kuei was flushing with embarrassment at his sharpness, said indignantly, 'I do not think it at all surprising people believe such things: why, these foreigners say openly that it's part of their religion to eat a man's flesh and blood! And our servant tells me there are even godwomen!' She gave a shudder of half pleasurable horror at the thought; how she would love to see such a monster for herself!

Han-lao smiled at her, pleased that these days she took talk about Boxers so much in her stride. 'There are indeed, and the stories about them are just as gruesome. The latest one is that the godwomen's passion for collecting unwanted children into orphanages is so that they can cut out their eyes and hearts to make into Western medicines! The only flaw in the Boxers' argument there is that every orphanage is bursting at the seams with perfectly healthy children, as Lan-kuei knows for herself, since Sung asked her to inspect one for him.'

'Oh!' Ko-chin stared furiously at Lan-kuei's suddenly smug face. Why should she be denied such a modern experience when a luke-warm reformer like Lan-kuei —oh, it was too bad! The moment their guests had gone, she cried, 'My husband, I am sixteen years old, with unbound feet, yet you do not trust me as your friend does his wife! Only today she told me that, since he is too busy to attend, she goes to see the latest street play rousing the people against the foreigners. Never have I seen a play—or a foreigner!'

Han-lao opened his mouth, then closed it again as she sank to his feet and lifted imploring eyes. 'My lord,' she urged softly, 'think, if the Boxers should come, I may never again have the chance to do such a thing!'

Unable to see how he could reasonably refuse, Han-lao muttered, 'Well, I suppose so long as your sedan stays close to Lan-kuei's and you remain hidden . . . but remember, wife, the streets are rough places. Take every care, for my sake if not your own.'

Ko-chin's heart was already fluttering with excitement—and fear. If only it were over and she were safely back home again! She could settle to nothing and when at last Han-lao handed her into her curtained sedan his face was sombre; it hadn't been pleasant, seeing her so absorbed these last few days in thoughts of her own, and now seeing her off like this on an independent expedition went bitterly against the grain.

Ko-chin noticed nothing, though, outside her own needle-sharp tension which heightened every sensation almost unbearably—was this how a person felt after smoking an opium pipe? Almost, for a moment, she felt this journey was worse than her last by sedan, to her wedding with Han-lao; but then the bearers turned out of the narrow lane into a crowded street and she forgot everything except the extraordinary scenes unfolding outside her tiny window on the world. So much light—colour—noise! It was a mind-shattering kaleidoscope to eyes and ears accustomed to shade and stillness but, as the bearers forged their way steadily through the seething streets, her racing heart calmed a little. It would be ungracious of a woman of the world such as she was becoming to forget her promise to a little, home-bound sister . . . Ko-chin interrupted the bearers' melancholy cry—'I borrow your light!'—with an order to stop at the nearest stall to buy the candied arbutus Mo-ch'o so loved.

Then they went jolting on over the uneven streets, slipping sometimes on pools of slime that oozed up from the choked drains, until at last Ko-chin heard Lan-kuei's voice calling from a sedan alongside, 'Is all well with you, my friend?'

In an excited squeak, Ko-chin called back, 'Very well, I thank you! But why are we stopping here?'

'We have arrived and the play is starting!'

Ko-chin had forgotten about the play. With a guilty start, she peeped at the crowd gathering to watch the monstrous creature strutting forward on a makeshift stage. 'Do not be afraid, my friend,' she heard Lan-kuei hiss, 'it's only an actor pretending to be a foreign devil.'

Even so—Ko-chin's breath came very fast as the monster roared, 'We foreign devils are creeping into every corner of your land and you Chinese know better than most what death and terror invasion brings! Remember the Huns—the Mongols—the Tartars—'

Suddenly the stage was seething with impossible, hideously grimacing monsters and Ko-chin's wail of terror was lost in the crowd's frenzied howl of hatred for past despoilers. But even above that howl the monster's voice could be heard, shrieking, 'You built your Great Wall to protect yourselves but a hundred walls won't keep us out!'

'Exterminate all barbarians!' screamed a single voice from the crowd. 'See, they even spy on us here!'

Ko-chin's head whipped round to glimpse a foreign godwoman with a cluster of converts at the corner of the square. Then the bewildered little group was swamped by the crowd. 'They'll try to force her up on to the stage,' gasped Lan-kuei. 'We must leave, Ko-chin.'

Ko-chin sat motionless: how quickly the gods granted wishes you hadn't really meant! There was a foreign devil right in front of her, and only she could save it! Because even such a hysterical mob as this wouldn't dare attack the sedan of so powerful a man as Han-lao's uncle—would they? So, if she could get the creature inside the sedan . . . heart pounding, Ko-chin waited until it was within arm's length, then leaned out snapping, 'In here!'

Heaven be thanked, the creature did not hesitate. With one scramble she was inside and immediately the bearers, cursing but obedient to Ko-chin's sharp command, heaved up the sedan and set off at a stumbling run. Ko-chin's relief was shortlived. She hadn't thought how, in the narrow sedan, she would be disgustingly, unbearably squashed against this ghoulish creature from another world. Her nostrils full of the rank odour of foreign flesh, she cringed away, ignoring the babble of raucous sounds it was making. It seemed an eternity before they reached a street quiet enough to push the creature out.

Now, Ko-chin considered, her duty as a modern woman was done; unfortunately, though, the foreign female didn't see it that way. She stumbled alongside, still mouthing strange sounds at Ko-chin. Ko-chin clenched the curtains together, wondering frantically how you made them go away? Perhaps the family gateman would know? But he didn't. The godwoman just pushed him aside and followed Ko-chin into the house.

Inside the safety of her own rooms Ko-chin really looked at the creature for the first time. How repulsive it was, with those fishy eyes in a pallid face and thin hair the colour of sand! Yet, unnatural though it was, it was undoubtedly human and Ko-chin felt a sharp pang of disappointment. She had expected something much more dramatic, after all the stories she had heard of foreign devils. Why, she even felt rather sorry for a sister-woman so astray, so ignorant of civilized behaviour! But by now she had seen enough of foreign devils. Ko-chin sighed with relief when she heard Han-lao coming, surely he would know the right language to make the godwoman go away.

He did. When she had been despatched he told Ko-chin warmly, 'Well done, my wife! You saved that lady from a very nasty situation, and I've had a chance to practise my English!'

'You are so clever, my husband,' murmured Ko-chin. Then, trying not to sound as smug as she felt, 'But what can her husband be thinking of, to let her so expose herself?'

Han-lao shrugged. 'Who knows? I have heard some foreign women never marry at all! Wife, do you know what she asked me? Permission to bring her converts here for protection if the Boxers reach Peking! To take such advantage of your courtesy! A pity the manners of foreigners are not as good as their science. But now, tell me, little wife, am I to expect more guests?'

Ko-chin giggled nervously. 'No more, my lord. I'm very glad to have been out but so much gladder to be safe home again! I'm afraid I saw very little of the play but maybe my other news for you will compensate . . . '

She drew close to him, then bit back angry words when the servant cleared his throat at the door. Sung had arrived, looking so savage-eyed that Ko-chin cried, 'Oh, our friend, did Lan-kuei not reach home safely?'

'My wife is safe enough,' he told her abruptly. 'I'm the one who needs help! Han-lao, I have just heard that one of our reform leaders who escaped to Japan has begun our struggle again there, where he is safely out of the Imperial reach.'

'But that is marvellous news,' cried Han-lao.

'Not if I'm the one who has to send the daily reports he wants on events here,' Sung scowled. 'You know how I hate writing. But you like it, my friend—you'd enjoy compiling all those dreary summaries and analyses he wants—so, I beg you, say you will do it for me!'

No sooner had Han-lao agreed than Sung whirled out again and Ko-chin said softly, 'Now we both have joyful tasks ahead, husband—you, your writing, and I—' She ducked her head shyly. '—I have happiness within me, dear husband.'

He stared down at her, still half lost in the wild dreams for the future: the reform movement alive again, in a safe haven! Himself to work for it—here at first, of course, but later, who knew? Maybe in Japan—'But this is no time to be tied down by a child,' he cried. 'Oh, I know I agreed, wife, that reformers should have children, but not now! Not on the brink of a war here and things to take us abroad later—'

Then he glimpsed her devastated face and knew he had spoilt what should have been the supreme moment of her life. 'Forgive me,' he cried, 'I spoke without thinking—'

But already she was stumbling out of the room, choking, 'At least send word to your parents. They will rejoice that we have fulfilled our duty to them and to your ancestors!'

As soon as Mo-ch'o heard her sister's sobs, she ran to her, gasping, 'Remember your child, sister! Such grief will surely damage him—'

'How did you know?' sobbed Ko-chin.

'Because you have been so happy, so kind of late,' Mo-ch'o said softly. 'I was so worried when you went into the city lest—'

'Hush!' Ko-chin seized her arm. 'It's unlucky to speak of what might have happened. Oh, believe me, I am done with these reformers! From now on, I shall think only of my son!'

That resolve she kept. Despite Han-lao's frustrated anger, all Ko-chin's time now went into preparing for the baby's birth. She took all the advice given by his interested relatives, stitched endlessly at exquisite baby clothes in the finest materials, all scarlet for joy. She refused to listen to the rumours of death and destruction crackling and spitting from the city outside as the Boxers, lighted spills to gunpowder, blazed towards the heart of the Empire. They made no more threats against the Imperial Family: now, Boxers and government turned a single face against the unbearable arrogance of foreigners and their Chinese Christian converts. But Ko-chin, gowned in wine red to hold her spirit safely to earth, was more interested in the baby shoes with tiger faces she and Mo-ch'o were making. 'Do you remember how, when we were young, we had to wear shoes of cotton with ragsoles?' she asked, smiling tenderly. 'How different it will be for my son!'

Mo-ch'o smiled back. 'See what else I have made him, sister!' Shyly she gave Ko-chin a minute satin cap decorated with tiny gold Buddhas.

Ko-chin was so delighted she hardly listened to Han-lao's news that evening. Beyond saying absently, 'Well, if the people are on the Boxers' side, how can we blame the

Emperor's aunt for wanting them on hers, too? I must speak to your honourable aunt about a wet nurse for our son . . . '

With a sigh, Han-lao left her; these days, it was like talking to a stranger.

As Ko-chin's whole being became more and more concentrated on her child, even Mo-ch'o, who understood, became frightened for her. Then, two moons before the birth was due, Ko-chin awoke knowing something was wrong. It was so dark—it must be the Hour of the Tiger, she thought bemusedly. Awkwardly she manoeuvred her swollen body out of bed and tiptoed into Mo-ch'o's room. But she was sound asleep and Ko-chin dared not rouse her too suddenly, in case her soul had wandered too far from her sleeping body to find its way home quickly. She must wake a servant . . . but it was too late. With a cry of agony Ko-chin fell to the floor. As her life began to bleed away, it carried with it a tiny body.

Mo-ch'o told her afterwards that first Han-lao had sent for the foreign doctor, then told her to fetch Mrs Li—'So none of the other relations would try the old remedy of filling your nose and mouth with cotton to stop any more of your spirit escaping, sister! Then he went himself to pay priests to beat gongs to call back your wandering soul, even though he knew it would be the young foreign doctor who would save you—as he did, sister, Heaven be thanked!'

Ko-chin turned away indifferently. Of what use was that, when the Tiger of Night had eaten up her son?

CHAPTER 12

SONS

'What is this I hear?' Mrs Li looked sternly down at the slight form rigid under the satin coverlet, the white face and darkly shadowed eyes of her nephew's wife.

'The honourable lady must surely understand,' Ko-chin muttered sullenly. 'I am not strong enough yet to receive my husband.'

'Such nonsense.' Mrs Li sat down by the bedside. 'I am ashamed for you, Ko-chin. What cause has my nephew ever given you to treat him so?'

Ko-chin turned her face away, the pillow muffling her words: 'His mother was right—I am not worthy to be his wife. She will hate me even more now that I have lost her grandson.'

'But you misjudge your husband if you think he too hates you. He longs to see you, to comfort you. And, since I stand in place of his mother to you, I command that you receive him.'

However gentle Mrs Li's tone, Ko-chin knew an ultimatum when she heard one; no member of this household was allowed to mar the harmony of family life for long. Obediently she struggled up the bed, stammering, 'F-forgive me, honourable lady! I know I have forgotten myself, but—'

'But grief is great. I know, child, but we must not let it be our master. So, allow your sister to make you fit to be seen again.'

Already a servant was at the door with brass ewers of hot water. Another followed with red soap and towels. Mo-ch'o ran for Ko-chin's face powder and comb of white bone, discovered with a gasp of horror that there was no jasmine oil left—another servant was sent running to buy more. Within the hour Ko-chin was ready and Mo-ch'o, holding up a mirror for her sister, whispered, 'Your mother-in-law is far away—long before you see her you will have made another son!'

Then Ko-chin was left alone to wait for Han-lao. She wrung her hands together, thoughts rampaging. Reformer or not, he had every right to look for a second woman now—one who could bear sons. She froze—footsteps— the door-curtain swung aside. He had come, her fixed eyes met his; then he was beside her, clasping her shaking hands as he exclaimed, 'Dear wife, Heaven be thanked that you live! Though I suspect good Western doctoring had more to do with it than any god!' And then he was fastening a bracelet of jade and gold about her wrist.

An angry husband did not bring gifts to the wife who had failed him . . . strange how these last months, feeling herself a traditional wife at last, she had forgotten what he was really like. Maybe that had angered him more than losing his son? 'Oh, my dear lord,' she sobbed, 'does a modern woman need such things?'

'She does,' he told her softly, 'and only jade, fairest of stones, is fit for you.'

She was needed. For herself. The moment was too great for speech and huge pity for all those women not married to a modern man nearly overwhelmed Ko-chin. To be so close in understanding to a husband was worth all the pains it caused. Han-lao wiped away her tears, then gave her his old shining smile as she faltered, 'You are too good to me, my husband. Next time I will do better, nor forget, as I have done of late, that I must learn how to be a good reformer as well as a mother!'

'All I ask for now is to see you strong again,' he returned gently. 'I will leave you to rest now, but later, perhaps you would care to read the draft of my latest report to Japan?'

'I am not tired, I will read it at once,' she said swiftly. Then, to hold him a little longer, 'But tell me, I beg you, husband, what is happening in the city?'

Han-lao sat down again at once, only too happy to oblige; he had missed Ko-chin's instant and rapt attention very badly over the past weeks. 'Well, the Boxers have changed their slogan to, "Uphold the Great Pure Dynasty and exterminate the barbarians!" As a reward for that about-face, the Emperor's aunt has punished an official who executed a bunch of them as murderous trouble-makers.'

'But Boxers say bullets can't hurt them!' Ko-chin gasped. 'Surely they did not die?'

'They died,' grinned Han-lao, 'but that hasn't damaged their reputation; it's generally agreed that, if the bodies were as dead as they looked, then their owners had never been real Boxers in the first place!'

Ko-chin managed a shadowy smile at that but she didn't want to think about Boxers. 'And the Emperor?' she whispered.

'He has been made to admit before a special audience that he can never father a son himself—and so craves of his aunt that she selects a worthy Heir Apparent to succeed. The ultimate humiliation.'

Ko-chin was silent for a moment, then she said quietly, 'Poor man. But, as your friend the Prince Sung told us, it is of ourselves we must think now. Go back to your work, dear husband, and have no fear for me—I shall soon be well.'

Ko-chin kept that promise but, in the icy winter weeks that followed, she often wondered if she had imagined the deep tenderness between them that day. By springtime she was certain that she had. 'If my husband is not out, he is at his desk writing,' she told Lan-kuei distractedly one late spring day, when all the world outside was surging with new life. 'He never so much as smiles at me now, let alone stays to talk! Oh, my friend, can it be after all that he hates me for losing his son?'

Lan-kuei hesitated, torn between conflicting feelings. She hadn't been able to avoid a fierce pleasure when, miscarrying, this Chinese girl had failed in one thing at least, but on the other hand . . . very slowly Lan-kuei was coming to understand that women, whatever their race, should be kinder to one another, since they all suffered at the hands of men . . . Even so, the admission came hard: 'My husband is the same,' she said harshly. 'So grim, so angry all the time. But I do not ask what is wrong; better not to know!'

Ko-chin shook her head slowly. 'If we are to be made so miserable, I think we have the right to know why— especially when—' She ducked her head. '—oh, Lan-kuei, although I am well enough now to make another son, my husband never comes to my bed!'

'Nor my husband to mine,' Lan-kuei whispered back. It was the ultimate failure for a wife, and they stared at one another in mute misery.

Then Ko-chin rallied. 'Tomorrow, when my husband returns from the Boxer meeting, I shall ask what has changed him so,' she declared. 'We have that right!'

They were brave words but, had it not been for the letter which arrived the next morning from Han-lao's home, Ko-chin might have lost courage at the sight of Han-lao's closed face. He hardly seemed to see her, just brushed by with a few muttered words of greeting. 'As if I were part of the furniture,' she thought with sudden up-surging anger. 'My husband!' Jolted out of his thoughts, Han-lao turned. 'Your honourable mother commands that we return to her, that she may be sure no more sons are lost.'

'Sons?' muttered Han-lao, eyes blank. Then his face flushed scarlet. 'SONS!' he roared. 'Why should I breed more people, when every day I pray the beastliness and savagery of men may be wiped from the earth!'

Ko-chin staggered backwards, stumbling against a chair as he advanced on her to seize her shoulders and shake her furiously. A devil must have possessed him! 'Sister, help me,' she screamed. But, as Mo-ch'o stumbled through the doorway, Han-lao violently pushed her away from him. Falling into a chair, he buried his head in his arms, shoulders heaving. Mo-ch'o fled, leaving Ko-chin kneeling beside her husband; now that the crisis had come, she was completely in command of herself.

When at last his terrible dry sobbing eased, she said quietly, 'My husband, these past weeks you have kept me from your company: I am left empty, mind and body, and I can stand it no longer. I beg you, tell me what is wrong.'

Han-lao raised bleared eyes. 'Only that I have discovered what a coward I am—that at the first scream of a victim I want to run!' Stumblingly then, as Ko-chin wiped the tears from his face with the sleeve of her gown, he told her, 'The Boxers do as they like now they have Imperial backing! And to make my reports to Japan I have to yell "Burn, burn, burn—kill, kill, kill!" with the villagers— smell the stench when the Boxers herd the local converts into huts and burn them alive—which is kind compared to what they do to some of them—oh, Ko-chin, every meeting is an orgy of torture and killing and anyone who tries to stop the slaughter is chopped into little pieces!' Blindly he stretched out his arms to her. 'Oh, wife, I wish I were dead!'

Gently she rocked him, murmuring, 'But you will be brave and live, because you are a man and can *change* things—as you changed my life. Listen, my husband, if it had not been for you, I would have been dead long ago.'

He jerked away from her. 'You mean you would have killed yourself if you had been sent to old Chen?' Then, when she nodded calmly, 'but you were still a child!'

'A toy of no value, to be thrown away when broken. I preferred to break my body myself, husband, since, before there were men like you, that was the only free action left to us women.' Ko-chin leaned towards him: 'But now, my husband, I am a person, not just a thing to be used! I will not give that up easily—nor you—nor the chance to make more men like you!'

Han-lao let her help him to his feet and she called to Mo-ch'o to bring tea. When she had filled his tea-bowl, she went on thoughtfully, 'You are so afraid at the Boxer meetings, I think, because you know yourself helpless and men find that hard to bear. But if you knew how to fight back . . . do you remember our friend Sung speaking of making good soldiers when I listened from behind a screen —oh, many months ago!'

'I'm not likely to forget the first time you ever spoke out for yourself, little wife!' he told her, almost smiling, and, seeing his eyes come back to life again, Ko-chin relaxed a little.

Smiling herself, she asked softly, 'So how do we stop it being true to say "poor iron for nails, poor men for soldiers"?'

He frowned. 'Well, first of all we have to change our whole idea of what a soldier is,' he muttered. 'I can see now how stupid we reformers have been, thinking we could build a modern army just by giving up-to-date firearms to the usual horde of criminals we call soldiers. But, wife, in all of history there can never have been the kind of army we need!'

'We need an army to fight not just against invaders but against all the cruelty and poverty and misery that both men and women suffer in our land,' she cried, eyes shining into his.

Han-lao stood up, drawing her with him. 'And that means a whole new philosophy, a whole new army and, one day, a whole new way of living,' he declared huskily. 'That is a dream worth living for, my wife.'

And the nightmare shadows fled his eyes as he began, with her, to plan an army such as there had never been before—a people's army.

CHAPTER 13

'BURN AND KILL!'

Fight back? Brave words in springtime seemed hideously ironic in the scorching summer days that followed when, with Boxers snapping at their heels, endless streams of godmen and their converted 'Secondary Devils' poured into the city for refuge.

'Why do they come?' Mo-ch'o cried wildly. 'There's no help for them here—the Emperor's aunt wants them dead. And they deserve to die—if it wasn't for them, there wouldn't be any Boxers!'

She ran indoors, leaving Ko-chin alone in the cool little courtyard where they sat now at nights waiting for Han-lao to come home. Ko-chin, her face a pale oval in the uneasy moonlight, shivered: what would happen to her little sister's scattering wits when she heard that yesterday Han-lao had seen the first Boxers actually inside the city walls? Even men thought twice before they went out these days, when Manchu Bannermen draped in tigerskins, with tigers' heads mounted on their shields, strutted the streets, licking their lips over the killing to come.

Ko-chin was bitterly disappointed that Han-lao hardly seemed to hear when she told him that a new life had begun within her; yet even herself, now that the main force of the Boxers was so very nearly here, she could feel no real happiness. Many of those Boxers were scarcely more than children themselves, Han-lao told her, biting his lips; tatterdemalion creatures with red scarves around necks, ankles and wrists, and the character for 'happiness' emblazoned on their chests—'when their hands are red with blood.' Over her dead body, thought Ko-chin, would Han-lao go out again once they were inside the city . . . oh, if only he would come home!

But first she heard Sung's footsteps. 'I told him to stay indoors,' he stormed when she told him Han-lao was not yet back. 'I can't wait for him, my friend's wife, but tell him from me: tomorrow a large force of Boxers enters the city. Make him understand that streets awash with blood are no place for would-be journalists.'

Then she was alone again. Reaching out a hand to the cool jade of her little Goddess of Mercy, Ko-chin lifted her eyes to the small square of captive, distant stars above their courtyard, praying not only for her husband and his family but also for all those others, of so many different races, trapped tonight inside the layered city walls. Above all, though, she prayed for the safety of her unborn child.

At first the household was bewildered by the strange dull roar that began at dawn the next day. Outside in their own courtyard, though, Han-lao soon guessed what it was: thousands of panic-stricken voices mingling with the pounding of their feet from the narrow streets outside; but the noise of their terror could not drown out the rhythmic, raucous chant of the Boxer hordes who pursued them: 'Burn, burn, burn! Kill, kill, kill!'

Han-lao raced for the family gate to the street, Ko-chin hard on his heels. There, they could see for themselves the seething torrent of men, women, children, animals, desperate to escape. The red dust, blown into the city by summer winds from far-off deserts, whirled up in clouds around them, heavy with the reek of their fear. When the first death scream came from the road ahead of them, they tried to turn—children and women stumbled, fell, were trampled down—Han-lao slammed the gate on the muddy soup of humanity, choking, 'The killing has begun.' Gathering Ko-chin to him, he pressed his hands over her ears. Behind her, she could feel Mo-ch'o's clutching hands and the three of them stood welded together until the first arcs of flame scarred the hot blue sky above them and the bitter tang of smoke stung their nostrils. Then they staggered indoors.

The night was as noisy as the day, although by then the crash of falling masonry and rending rafters from all around drowned out the screams of the dying. Han-lao paced the floor until first light. Then he went out into the smoking, silent city, wrenching his sleeve from Ko-chin's frenzied grip. Sobbing, she watched him run down the street; his feet did not stir the blood-sodden dust. 'He would not listen to me,' she moaned, as gentle arms encircled her.

'Come indoors, little one,' Mrs Li said gently, 'and be calm; it is not for you to command your husband, however ill-judged his actions.'

'He says he has to write down what has happened, not just for his report to Japan,' Ko-chin sobbed, 'but to bear witness for the future—oh, this I cannot bear!'

Mrs Li's voice was suddenly stern: 'You have no choice, so bear it with dignity. But you may sit with me until your husband returns.'

They were the longest hours in Ko-chin's life. When at last a servant stumbled into the room, gasping to Mrs Li, 'Honourable Lady, your nephew has returned but—aiya! —in such a state—' she did not wait for permission to go to him. Her flying feet only stopped when she had Han-lao's battered, reeking body in her arms. With the servant's help she got him to his bed, peeled away the soot-grimed gown, wet with huge dark stains, to reveal the bullet wound in his shoulder. As they dealt with that, Han-lao muttered and moaned, eyes rolling beneath the swollen lids.

'He has fever, lady,' said the servant. 'We need the foreign doctor!'

'If any foreigner steps from the Legation Quarter where he must live, he will be murdered this night,' Ko-chin told him thickly. 'Fetch herbs! And take this away!'

She thrust the stinking gown, heavy with polluted smoke, into his arms and turned back to Han-lao. As she tried to bathe his battered face, though, he seized her hand, gabbling, 'My wife—I can't find her! Out there, in all that blood! Boxers dripping with it—bodies everywhere—ears, noses cut off! Don't let them get Ko-chin! She mustn't see the eyes gouged out like shiny black grapes!—Help us!'

It was thirty-six hours before Han-lao's fever broke and, long before they ended, Ko-chin's mind grew numbed by his catalogue of horrors. At the Hour of the Tiger, the hour when Death had carried their child on to the Terrace of Night, when at last she knew that he would live, he whispered, 'Have I been talking?' Ko-chin did not dare to trust her voice but, in the flickering light from the bean-oil lamp, he knew from her eyes that for her, too, the shadows thronged with the hungry ghosts of the newly slaughtered. Then, like a lost child he cried, 'How shall we go on living, knowing what we know of men?'

Ko-chin summoned up the last of her strength: 'Only by remembering, my husband, that there is a best as well as a worst—that there *are* good people. Your uncle, aunt, your friend the Prince Sung, and his friend who married my sister to save her—and *you*! This madness will pass. Then the voices of the sane will be heard again . . .'

Her voice broke and they wept together, knowing that, whatever happened, they could never be the same people again.

For two days after the mayhem, uncanny silence cocooned the Boxer-infested city but, on the third day, a hammering at the gates threw the old gateman into a frenzy of terror. Gently Han-lao's uncle told him, 'It is the turn of our household to be checked by the Boxers for any taint of the foreign religion. Open the gates, because if you do not they will burn them down. My wife is already gathering the household together in the guest hall.'

On the side of the room where the women stood, the greens and pinks, apricots and blues of silken gowns made rich pools of colour in the subdued light filtering through rice-papered lattices, but every face was deathly pale. Across the room, Ko-chin could see Han-lao propped between two cousins, but even as she thought, 'Rising from his bed so soon will bring back the fever,' the old gateman was propelled into the room, a knife at his throat. Behind him pressed Boxers, fresh blood dripping from their sodden clothes on to the pale grey tiles of the floor.

The smoke-hoarsened voice of their leader ripped the breathless silence: 'Have any here eaten the foreign religion?'

'None,' came the calm reply. Tall and spare in his grey brocaded silk robe, leaning on his staff of ebony and silver, Han-lao's uncle was every inch scholar and gentleman. Surely even a Boxer would believe him?

Then Ko-chin's brain jolted in her skull: it was at *her* the gateman pointed as he screamed, 'That one—she brought a foreign she-devil into the house!' Then, brokenly, 'Forgive me, my master! They swore they would kill my old wife if I did not tell them something!'

'Just like this,' snarled the Boxer who held him pinioned. And with a ghastly grin he slit the old man's throat from ear to ear. The mesmerized family watched him die, then their eyes swivelled back to Ko-chin.

Han-lao's uncle swayed. 'What nonsense has my old fool of a gateman told you?' he muttered.

'You ask that? The goings-on there are under your roof?'

From behind the Boxers a new figure stepped, unkempt but not blood-stained; in some things, the ex-reformer Ting-i was fastidious.

'You!' Han-lao staggered forward, one hand clasped to his injured shoulder. 'So you have found your true level at last, son of old Chen!'

The Boxers edged into a circle around the two young men as Ting-i, lips drawn back over his yellowed teeth, hissed, 'That woman you stole was my father's meat, Han-lao, as was her sister. At least he shall have the heads of his rightful property in recompense!'

Mo-ch'o slid in a senseless heap at Ko-chin's feet as Ting-i advanced towards them. Grasping Ko-chin's chin he sneered, 'My only fear is that your blood will sully their swords, prostitute of reformers!' Then he gargled as the edge of Han-lao's hand caught him full force across the throat and he dropped like a stone. Even as the first sword whistled towards Han-lao's neck he fell too, so that it cut only air. Ko-chin threw herself over his prostrate body as, in the one split second left, a deep voice spoke from the doorway.

'Pardon me for interrupting, but why do you waste time here, when everywhere there are Secondary Devils still alive?'

As one man, the wild-eyed band swung round. Eyeball to eyeball, the newcomer and the Boxer leader weighed one another. But Sung, in the full military uniform of a Manchu Prince, was a daunting figure. Before his one drawn sword, the others dropped. Then he snarled, 'This family is personally known to me as incorruptible, and murdering families known to be loyal to the Dynasty is not one of your duties. Now out—and be grateful I do not report your names to the authorities.'

They slunk away and Sung strode across to lift Ko-chin from Han-lao's body.

Her voice lifted hysterically. 'Does my husband live, our friend?'

'He lives, my friend's wife,' Sung's deep voice answered.

He did not speak again until Han-lao was safely back in his bed. Then he murmured, 'Really, Han-lao, the company you keep when I'm not with you is quite shocking!'

The lightness of his voice was in stark contrast, though, to his smouldering eyes and harsh-set mouth. With shaking hands, Ko-chin somehow made tea and faltered: 'Will you honour us, our friend, by accepting a bowl of Cloud Mist Tea from high Kiangsi? It is our poor best, kept for special occasions . . . '

Her voice trailed away and, when he did not answer, she turned to leave the room. Only then did he rouse himself to growl, 'Forgive me, friends. But, in truth, I am ashamed to speak to you—'

'When we owe you our lives?' scoffed Han-lao weakly.

Sung only buried his face in his hands. 'What are two lives saved by one Manchu,' he muttered through his fingers, 'when last night I watched my brother Manchus touring the city, chortling at the sight of thousands of Chinese being cut into little pieces?'

So he had been out in the slaughter . . . terrible as it was to see him weep, Ko-chin's heart eased a little; truly this was a good man. And when at last he raised his wet face to tell them, 'I can't endure the farce of my life here any longer—if we survive the next few weeks, which I doubt, I shall leave for Japan,' she breathed, 'And your wife?'

He turned away. 'I don't know. We quarrelled—she said she would never live in exile with half-crazed revolutionaries.'

'More to the point, will the half-crazed revolutionaries accept *you*, a Manchu?' Han-lao asked carefully.

Sung shrugged. 'When their leader, Dr Sun Yat-sen, realizes how much inside information I can give him, I think he'll make me an exception to his anti-Manchu stand. So—' He seized his teabowl. '—here's to revolution, my friends, because I know now it will take nothing less to cure what's wrong with our country. Why not come with me? There's nothing left here we can do.'

Ko-chin caught her breath as Han-lao looked up sharply. 'I could take my last report with me,' he said slowly, then looked at Ko-chin. 'But my wife—I do not know.'

Ko-chin gave a heartbroken cry and hastily Sung said, 'Rest and recover for now, my friends. And—' He laughed unpleasantly. '—be sure I will deal with that worm Ting-i on your behalf !'

Old Chen's son. Ko-chin fixed agonized eyes on Han-lao as, after Sung had gone, he tried to explain to her: 'You see, my wife, I used to think you would be safe with any reformer—as if mere ideas could change the nature of a man! But since that day Ting-i brought T'an here, I've wondered—have I been wrong to expose you the way I have? And how can I be sure that revolutionaries, with their bomb-making and wild ideas, aren't even less fit to be with a respectable woman?'

'How should one dishonourable man's insults make me less respectable in the eyes of honourable men?' Ko-chin cried passionately. 'And only Ting-i of all the reformers ever insulted me!'

'Is not one enough?' Han-lao flashed back. 'But I'm not talking about insults—I'm talking about your life—if you had died today, Ko-chin, it would have been my fault!'

'I would rather have died than be left behind now,' she sobbed.

He lay back weakly on his pillow, muttering, 'That is foolish, wife, for how then would you give me those soldier sons you have promised me?'

Could he have forgotten? 'But we already have our first son growing inside me,' she cried, 'so you cannot leave me behind!'

His eyes dropped. 'Of course,' he muttered. 'That is good, for my mother will receive you with open arms. And be sure, wife, as soon as I know that it is safe for you in Japan, I will send for you and the child.'

Ko-chin knew then she had lost him. So far away, engrossed in a new struggle, he would never think of her. When, the next day, Boxer fires spread to engulf the great triple-towered Emperor's Gateway, she did not care. So its destruction was said to foretell the end of the Dynasty—what did that matter, when her own world had collapsed? When the fallen Emperor's aunt instructed her armies, with the Boxers in the vanguard, to besiege the foreign ambassadors in their Legation Quarter, she officially declared war upon the world—a war she had no more hope of winning than Ko-chin had of changing Han-lao's mind, poisoned by the son of old Chen. Lan-kuei had been right: men weren't really interested in changing anything for women, so they might as well kill each other once and for all.

CHAPTER 14

FISH IN THE STEWPAN

The next two months Ko-chin would always remember as the worst weeks in her life. Ears assaulted by the endless booming of guns; lungs gagging at air saturated with the stench of putrifying Boxer bodies, shot down as they hurled themselves at the Legation Quarter's hastily erected defences; every surface polluted by the fat flies that bred in their millions on the piled flesh left to rot around the Legation Quarter, where the besieged foreigners fought to fend off their attackers until an international rescue force could reach them. But worst of all to bear was the deadly depression that had settled on her since she had known she must return to her mother-in-law.

She listened drearily as Sung, who had dared the dark streets one night to bring them news, reported, 'The Emperor's aunt rages because her armies can't break the siege—what she doesn't know is that, in the hope that the international rescue force won't raze this city from the face of the earth when it arrives, her army generals are deliberately firing too high.'

'So her boast that she has the foreigners trapped like fish in a stewpan—' began Han-lao.

'Is worthless,' cut in Sung, 'for as long as her generals can deceive her. If the siege is broken and what's left of the Boxers let loose on the foreign ambassadors and their families—'

He broke off with a shrug and Ko-chin shuddered. Why did she waste energy worrying about the future, when they were so unlikely to have one? Huddled on her chair, she reminded Sung of a small, storm-driven bird and he tried to inject some cheerfulness into his voice as, rising to leave, he declared, 'But on the bright side, my friends, this siege is a marvellous way of ridding ourselves of Boxers—a point of view I suspect our generals heartily share!'

'Well, I wish they would arrange to have their corpses cleared up,' said Han-lao, disgustedly swatting at the huge fly trying to settle on his teabowl rim. 'Otherwise, in this heat, even the residents of the Forbidden City will be dying in epidemics.'

'Oh, their Imperial Majesties will run before they take any fatal harm,' Sung told him abruptly. 'I gather from my wife that even the Emperor's aunt is dismayed by the way the Boxers' so-called magical powers have let her down. She's talking now about the need to make a "Tour of Inspection", to check on the conduct of city officials at a convenient distance from Peking!' Nobody smiled, so after an awkward moment he went on, 'Now I must see your uncle, Han-lao—it's imperative that, when the international rescue force does arrive and take over, you all stay put. Foreign soldiers under disciplined leadership will leave you alone so long as you don't get in their way, but our own hungry, footloose soldiers and Boxers won't be so scrupulous.'

It was hard advice to take when, the night after the foreign soldiers had arrived, they watched the people of Peking fleeing: through a crack in the gate, Ko-chin and Mo-ch'o could see for themselves the loaded carts, mules, camels—all being driven out of the city. 'Oh, sister,' sobbed Mo-ch'o, 'surely we should go too! Who knows what the foreign devils will do to us women when they have killed the men of the household?'

But before Ko-chin could answer she felt their servant tug at her sleeve. 'Come quickly, lady,' he hissed. 'The Manchu princess has dared the streets to come here in her sedan—and I think her wits are gone!'

At first, Ko-chin thought so, too. Never before had they seen Lan-kuei like this—gown rumpled, half-tumbled hair in draggles around her face, dark rivulets streaking her thick make-up, 'Oh, our friend,' screamed Mo-ch'o, 'a foreign devil has attacked you!'

Lan-kuei didn't answer, just stumbled to a chair as Han-lao, who had come running at Mo-ch'o's scream, asked sharply, 'Our friend, where is your husband? He should be with you—'

'Why so? He cares nothing for me,' Lan-kuei muttered, eyes straying around the quiet room. Why had she come here? She couldn't remember—'Rest, our friend,' she heard dimly, and a steaming teabowl was held to her lips. The heat helped: so much vomiting had left her cold and empty.

This time, when Han-lao demanded, 'Lan-kuei, tell us, what has happened in the Forbidden City to drive you here alone and in such distress?' she muttered, 'Nothing happens there. The Imperial Family have gone—some of them.'

Lan-kuei shuddered. Why not make the day of these two stupid, innocent Chinese as vile as it was for her? Voice queerly high-pitched, she found her tongue: 'Before light this morning, Her Majesty ordered her six-inch-long finger nails cut as short as any peasant's. Then she was dressed in peasant's clothes of dark blue and her hair bound up in a cotton scarf. When that was done, she went herself to fetch her nephew. Eunuchs stripped off his pearl-studded robes and red-tasselled hat and dressed him like a peasant, too.'

Lan-kuei giggled hysterically at the memory. How ordinary their Imperial Majesties had looked, stripped of their finery! No danger of the foreign devils recognizing them on their way out of Peking . . . 'They left through the Gate of the Virtue of Victory. There was such a crowd,

I couldn't see much, but when the Pearl Concubine came I could hear what the fool said—'

Lan-kuei broke off. Would she ever be able to wipe those words from her mind? For, in a voice rusty from long disuse, the Pearl had spoken words she must have known could never be forgiven. Wonderment mingled with bitterness in Lan-kuei's tone as she repeated them now for these Chinese: '"Your Majesty," the fool said, "know that you everlastingly dishonour the Dynasty if you take the Son of Heaven from his people like a thief in the night! Stay, to face the enemy and save the honour of the Empire!" I—I didn't hear any more—everyone was shouting—but they're saying Her Majesty was so enraged that—'

'What?' cried Ko-chin, wringing her hands in anguish.

'She ordered the Pearl Concubine to be thrown down a well. They say the Emperor grovelled at his aunt's feet, pleading for mercy but—'

Han-lao reached for Ko-chin as she swayed where she stood, but she pushed his hands away. If this was true, there could be no return to light and life for the Pearl Concubine who had become so real to her. She would have died as Ko-chin knew she had lived the long months of her imprisonment—mute but with her soul ablaze.

Lan-kuei, glaring, pushed past Han-lao to seize Ko-chin's shoulders and shake her furiously, shouting, 'Why grieve for that fool? If she had been loyal to her own race she would never have allowed the Emperor to be corrupted by reformers, and he would never have flouted his aunt—we could all have lived in peace if it wasn't for the likes of you! Oh, never will I cross your threshold again . . . !'

Ko-chin gazed at her aghast. Yet she understood. Lan-kuei had been shocked to the roots of her soul. Whether that hideous rumour was true or not, the Manchu girl would never be the same again. And just now she didn't know what she was saying—Ko-chin rushed after her, gasping, 'I beg you, at least wait with us, my friend—allow us to send for your husband to take you home.'

'Home?' spat Lan-kuei. 'What home, when my husband plans to desert me since I have refused to join the enemy with him in another land?'

Paler than ever, Ko-chin cried, 'Lan-kuei, you cannot believe we are your enemies!'

Lan-kuei ignored Ko-chin's outstretched hands, muttering, 'All those who expect me to forgo the luxury and privilege I was born to are my enemies.'

'So at heart you care nothing for anyone else—or our cause. Only for yourself, the princess,' said Ko-chin numbly. 'Then perhaps it is best you do go now. This humble Chinese home is unworthy to receive so honourable a visitor.'

Drearily Lan-kuei followed her to the door, her rage burnt out. 'One day, maybe, you will understand, Ko-chin,' she murmured, 'and forgive me for being too much of a coward not to be a princess; to face the things people can do to you if you are a nobody.' Then she was gone and the only sound to break the silence in the room was Mo-ch'o's sobbing.

When Sung came later that day, he told them Lan-kuei had chosen to follow the Imperial Family into exile. 'She learnt nothing from the example of the Pearl Concubine,' he added bitterly.

'That's exactly what she did do,' cried Ko-chin passionately. 'I wonder how brave you men would be if, when you spoke out of turn, you could be thrown down a well! We cannot go to Japan and begin again—it is the past or nothing for us!'

Sung raised his brows at this amazing breach of manners by his friend's usually impeccable wife but he only said, 'But my wife could have come with me, begun a new life.'

He glanced at Han-lao, sitting with his face turned away, then added softly, 'Understand, then, how hard it is for a man who has been a reformer to see his wife choose to continue in the service of a woman who considers having beaten to death the eunuch hairdresser who accidentally tweaked out two of the Imperial hairs. Now, Han-lao, tell me, are our wives, Manchu or Chinese, likely to deal with worse people abroad than they do at home?'

'My mother cannot be compared to the Emperor's aunt,' Han-lao told him stiffly. 'When I commit my wife to her protection, I shall explain the way a modern woman must be treated. And, with a son in her arms, I think my wife's reception will be warm enough.'

'My congratulations,' murmured Sung as Ko-chin blushed, and there was an awkward silence until she blurted, 'Have all in the city save this family fled into the countryside?' It was an uncanny thought.

Sung laughed harshly. 'A few hundreds are left but some of them are dangling from ropes, overcome by the disgrace of surrender to foreign devils. And their women, left unprotected, are throwing themselves down the wells so fast there will soon be no water fit to drink in the whole of Peking.'

To take such desperate leave of life! When Sung had gone, Ko-chin's legs refused to hold her up any longer. First Boxers, now barbarians free to pillage the Forbidden City. The great old house around her felt no stronger than an eggshell. Even the unaccustomed silence frightened her; stupid, now that the air no longer seemed about to ignite from heat and noise, to be unable to stop listening—listening for a sudden scream to rip that silence, to tell them the foreign devils were on the rampage.

But there were no screams, only unbroken silence. Sung had been right—so long as they kept within doors the foreign soldiers would not trouble them. Slowly summer passed into autumn and the child inside her grew. Ko-chin never doubted that it would be another son and already she and Han-lao were making plans for him—even though they both knew their hearts were empty of hope for the future. In that blazing, bloody summer, that had left a quarter of a million dead in the city, Han-lao had lost his old faith in people. And I, she thought dully . . . she blinked to keep back the tears; she must think of her son, not herself, from this time on. Swallowing hard, she asked, 'Has there been no news from outside today, my husband?'

Han-lao looked up from his book. 'Only that the foreign troops are having a fine time in the Forbidden City, squabbling over the Imperial treasures.'

'Good,' snapped Ko-chin. 'I hope the Emperor's aunt comes back to find nothing!'

Han-lao sighed. 'If what I hear is true, she wasn't so anti-foreign that she doesn't have a vast sum safely tucked away in a foreign bank. But—' Suddenly he chuckled. '—the foreign commanders have forbidden her to return here until she has been seen to punish the Boxers and their supporters! So no doubt she'll soon be requesting a lot of her former allies to take hasty leave of life!'

'But will she?' breathed Ko-chin.

'She has already begun. One of her recent hosts was told pointedly that the price of coffins was going up—he took the hint and hanged himself! And the Emperor has issued a Penitential Decree taking all the blame himself for the inconvenience the Boxers have caused to foreigners.'

'But, even if she would, she cannot bring the Pearl Concubine back to life,' Ko-chin whispered.

Han-lao scowled. 'The Pearl has been granted posthumous honours for her courage in drowning herself when she failed to catch up with the Imperial Caravan,' he said abruptly. 'For preferring death to dishonour at the hands of foreign devils, you understand. Ah, good, I see I have made you angry—anything rather than the hopeless apathy you show to everything else these days.' He raised a hand at her swift protest. 'Yes, even to our son.'

Stung beyond bearing, Ko-chin cried, 'And you, husband, who are you to talk of our son? So long as I have him, your conscience may rest easy about returning me to your mother!'

For a moment, she thought he would hit her. Still as a mouse, she watched him fight to regain control of himself. Then she went on quietly, 'Perhaps I have been too obedient a wife? But you made very clear what you wanted of me, my husband—that I should throw off the past and become a real person, find my self. It was very hard to do that, when all my life I had been taught that my own feelings were of no account—women have never been allowed selves! But, because I was so afraid you would send me back to your mother's courts, I had to try. For fear, not love!'

Ko-chin drew a long breath, seeing something very like fear in his own eyes at so much truth. For how many wives would obey their husbands if they had a choice? Their love had to be kept for sons, since husbands so rarely did anything to earn it! She laughed softly, telling him, 'But one day I was not afraid any more, my husband. I began to believe that, for the first time in my life, I could please myself a little—read, speak, think! That was when you became a person to me and I sought to please you no longer from fear but from love for what you are in yourself.'

She had never seen Han-lao rendered speechless by anyone before and she, a woman, had done it! Ko-chin sat back, exhausted by the longest speech of her life, reading his flabbergasted face like a book: he had wanted a modern wife; now he knew for certain that he had one and didn't know what to do about it! At last he muttered, 'For so long I thought I'd never be able to make you see me as more than an instrument to make you sons. But now—oh, can't you understand?' His voice rose passionately, 'How can I see a wife I love insulted by scum like Ting-i? Oh, wife, every night I dream he sends Boxers to hack you to pieces! There is so much evil in men—I did not know it before.'

'I think you did, husband,' Ko-chin told him quietly. 'Why otherwise did you become a reformer? From what you say, if you had not come to love me you would have let me continue to risk insult and death. Therefore, you are only sending me to your mother because you do not wish for other men to see me.' She rose to her feet, adding coldly, 'In which case, I might as well rebind my feet and become truly a wife in the old style; certainly my life hereon must be my son's, since you cannot after all give me my own life, husband.'

Han-lao sat in his chair all that night, the taste of failure scalding in his throat. She was more modern than he would ever be.

CHAPTER 15

EGGS OF HAPPINESS

When Ko-chin's time was only a few weeks away, she received an expected summons from Mrs Li. 'It will be to choose the wet-nurse for my son,' she said with relief to Mo-ch'o. 'I was beginning to fear she had forgotten!'

'Even the most important things get forgotten in these days,' muttered Mo-ch'o. 'Sister, I must ask you—'

But Ko-chin was already halfway to the door. 'When I return, little one! I must not keep my husband's aunt waiting.' But an uncomfortable pang of conscience struck her as she hurried away. How little she saw of Mo-ch'o these days—she did not even know in which part of the house her sister spent most of her time.

It seemed Mo-ch'o was on Mrs Li's mind too, from her first words: 'Ah, good, the little sister is not with you.'

'She is sewing for my child,' puffed Ko-chin, carefully lowering her swollen body on to a chair. Then she blurted, 'Oh, my husband's aunt, it is so difficult with my husband always at home now: because my sister refused to learn the new ways, he dislikes her . . . '

'Then how much more will her revolutionary husband despise her?' asked Mrs Li softly. 'Have you thought what is to become of your sister when you return to your mother-in-law?'

Ko-chin sat in shocked silence. How could she have forgotten? Mo-ch'o would have nowhere to go! 'Oh, lady,' she muttered, 'how selfish I have been! She has no place in the home of my husband's mother—but surely her husband's parents—?'

'They will not receive her,' Mrs Li replied gravely, 'because they do not recognize their son's marriage to her.

He was betrothed at birth to a friend's daughter, and they will not even grant your sister a concubine's rights to shelter. Perhaps now, Ko-chin, you will not feel yourself so badly treated: for, however little you may relish it, at least you have a safe haven.'

Ko-chin bit her lip. How insecure, how dangerous life was —Han-lao's anxiety about her was not all selfishness . . .

'You think of your husband,' murmured Mrs Li. 'He has, I think, won your heart as well as your mind, has he not? Ah, yes, I see it is so. You are much blessed, my nephew's wife.'

'I know it, honourable one,' whispered Ko-chin.

'Then you must forgive him if he fails in his promises to you now. I too am much disappointed for you, but my nephew must grow up a little more before he can realize that he will not lose you, just because other men find beautiful what he was taught should be for his eyes alone.'

'Even you, honourable lady, say "what", not "who",' said Ko-chin angrily. 'Am I still then only a thing, with no honour to call my own?'

Mrs Li raised her brows. 'How many men would keep their wives if the women were allowed any choice in the matter, little one? They are reared believing we must please them, not they us, and for that you must blame our history, not your husband.'

'The honourable lady is right to rebuke me,' Ko-chin faltered, remembering her father and brother, old Chen and his son. 'As for my sister, perhaps if I write to our own mother, a way could be found?'

'That I have already done. Your father refuses her, as is his right. My husband has therefore agreed that she should stay with us: there will be many such displaced ones, if our plans for change succeed, and we have a duty to succour those we know of.'

'Always you are gracious, lady,' gasped Ko-chin. 'I do not know how to thank you!'

'By not leaving my nephew more unhappy than you must,' Mrs Li told her softly. 'Now—' She clapped her hands and a servant came running, '—the wet-nurses for your child. We will inspect them.'

Ko-chin carefully studied the women who filed in to stand with bowed heads before her. This was an important choice; of course, Mrs Li would already have made sure each was strong and healthy, with enough milk to feed first Ko-chin's child, then her own, but character was important, too. Finally she chose a country girl with red cheeks and unbound feet, who seemed more intelligent than the rest.

Mrs Li rose. 'Now I will come with you to tell your husband what we have arranged. For you must know, Ko-chin, that had you not been returning to my nephew's mother, I would not have allowed you this wet-nurse. Nor do I think your husband will be pleased that I have engaged one.'

Was there no end to the shocks in this house, Ko-chin wondered dazedly. How could she be expected to feed the child herself and spoil her figure? It was her duty to her husband to keep her breasts beautiful! But to her dismay she found that Mrs Li was right: Han-lao was furious. Through gritted teeth, he demanded, 'My aunt, can this be right? For this is an evil custom! I know wet-nurses themselves are always fed well enough, because they must suckle the new son of a house, but how often are they refused the right to bring their own babies with them? More often than not they are left at home to slowly starve on a diet of thin gruel. That will not happen here, of course, but—'

'But do you intend to stay long enough in your parents' home to convert your mother to such new ways of thought?' Mrs Li interrupted smoothly. 'For, if you do not, your wife will pay the price of your principles.'

Ko-chin gripped the table edge, suddenly hysterical. 'Big feet—sagging breasts,' she cried, 'oh, how the women of your mother's courts will mock!'

Han-lao's eyes were naked with pain as they met hers. 'I know, believe me I know, my wife! I—'

But Ko-chin had gone. Her last week of waiting passed with deadly slowness, her mind as heavy as her body. When at last her time came, the labour was long before a living child wriggled and screamed between Mrs Li's strong slender hands.

'My son—let me see him,' panted Ko-chin, too weak to rise.

Mrs Li's voice was very gentle. 'My dear, a little girl, as pretty as a flower.'

A girl? 'No, I want my son,' whispered Ko-chin. It had to be a son. But it was not. When her wild despair had sunk into lassitude, Mrs Li said sternly, 'You are not saying you wish me to expose her?'

'I do not care what is done with her,' Ko-chin muttered, 'so long as she is taken away from me.'

Soon only Mo-ch'o was left beside her, holding the untasted bowl of brown sugar and water that new mothers must drink, and Ko-chin drifted into restless sleep. 'How sad it is . . . When a girl is born . . . ' Over and over the full hateful truth of those lines echoed through her dreams. Even their mothers had no reason to welcome them . . . Ko-chin awoke with a jerk. Had Mrs Li really exposed the baby? Sent her out to a baby-tower where unwanted infant girls were left to die? Oh, the little thing! Ko-chin wept, for herself, her baby girl, women everywhere. Givers of life, yet hated by gods and men alike—she did not understand why it had to be so . . .

The next time the child was brought to her, she put it to her breast; it was an act both of contrition and defiance.

Han-lao came once to stare at the child. He did not look at Ko-chin. 'I don't know what to do,' he muttered. She lay silent: she knew she would rather face a Boxer horde than her mother-in-law with only a daughter in her arms. He did not come again. It was Mo-ch'o who reminded her that her mother-in-law would be waiting for news. 'The eggs of happiness will be sent to her today,' said Mo-ch'o earnestly, 'but don't worry about it being an even number of eggs because it's a baby girl, sister! Your husband's aunt has told me that an even number is often sent for sons as well, to confuse evil spirits who might be jealous of a family's fortune. So that is what she is doing!' It was the best comfort she could offer.

The first day that Ko-chin left her bed Sung called, but a very different Sung, strong-boned face and heavy-lidded eyes as soft as they could ever be. 'A letter from my wife,' he announced, waving it in front of them, 'to tell me that at last, thanks to Her Dragon Majesty of all people, she understands! Listen to what she writes: "Husband, on our journey I have not only seen how everywhere the common people live in dirt, misery and hunger: I have experienced those things myself. On the first days of our journey, we had little food and no water—the Boxers have polluted all the wells with human heads. Yet at a government official's house this night, I have watched Her Majesty dine off myriad dishes served on gold and silver. I see now we cannot blame the foreign devils for all our ills, that we have to change ourselves . . . '

Sung broke off, laughing at their amazed faces. 'My friends, she has agreed to travel to Japan with me!' he ended triumphantly.

So the pride of the Manchu princess had been killed at last, thought Ko-chin bleakly. While she had to live out her life in age-old servitude to her mother-in-law, Lan-kuei would help to make a new world. The child's wail from the next room gave her a chance to excuse herself.

Pressed against Ko-chin's breast, the child blinked as a tear fell on her petal face. 'Oh, my little nameless one,' Ko-chin murmured, 'how can I bear to see your feet bound, a marriage arranged to a man we do not know? It would be better if we both—' But she shied away from that thought, even as a shadow darkened the doorway. 'Why, husband,' she faltered, 'has your friend gone so soon?'

Han-lao did not answer. Moodily he stared at the child and Ko-chin clutched it to her: 'I—I did not mean it, when I said she should be exposed—' she stammered.

Han-lao jumped. 'I should hope not, wife! Forgive me, I was thinking of the power mothers have to form a child's character. Do you remember, the very first time you spoke with Sung, deciding that it was because mothers spoilt their sons that our country had no decent soldiers? But, I have been thinking, if a mother taught all her children, sons and daughters alike, to think of others before themselves, that in itself would change the world!' Gently he took the child from her. 'And now we have a daughter ourselves, to teach how to become such a mother.'

We? Ko-chin breathed, 'How will we do that, my husband?'

He smiled down at her. 'How else but by teaching her to value herself? Only then will she be able to teach her sons to value others!'

Then, studying the tranquil, sleeping face in his arms, he added softly, 'But even with you for a mother she cannot learn so great a thing in my mother's courts.'

Could he really mean what she thought he meant? Ko-chin trembled but before he could say any more they heard Sung's voice outside, vibrant with urgency. Swiftly Han-lao passed the baby back to Ko-chin, exclaiming, 'What can have brought him back so soon?'

When they knew, they could hardly believe it, but Mo-ch'o's reaction to what Ko-chin had to tell her was very calm. All she said was, 'Then it is certain now that I have no place at all in the world.'

'Your husband would have had no time to think of you,' choked Ko-chin. 'He was killed outright by the bomb he was to throw . . . '

'Do not grieve for me, my sister,' Mo-ch'o told her in that same cool little voice. 'I have long wished to cut off my three thousand threads of trouble to enter the Doors of Emptiness. Now I may.'

So that was why Mo-ch'o had been so different, had prayed so often . . . how long had she been thinking of becoming a nun? Ko-chin was hot with shame, knowing that, ever since Mo-ch'o had come to this house, she had been too absorbed in her own problems to find out what her little sister was really thinking and feeling. And now it was too late: Mo-ch'o had turned her face from the world for ever. Ko-chin sobbed as she felt Mo-ch'o's touch on her arm, heard her whisper, 'There is no blame, sister. This is what I want, and your gift.'

'My gift?' cried Ko-chin.

'Your gift, because it is through you that I learnt that it is right to consider myself: if the parts of a whole are not in harmony, how can there ever be peace or justice? So think of me as one small piece of a great puzzle which has fallen into its rightful place, sister! And so I will have played my part.'

It was as though suddenly she was the elder, the wiser. Ko-chin said no more, although she wept when Mo-ch'o gave her the only gift she had ever received from her husband, a fan of silk and sweetly smelling sandalwood. Her hair would be returned later from the nunnery. After that, there would be no more little sister for Ko-chin but Mo-ch'o's eyes shone as, at their parting, she told her, 'We shall meet again when we pass to the Land of Extreme Felicity in the West, sister.'

When she had gone, Han-lao sat stroking Ko-chin's tear-stained cheeks. 'All lives cannot be the same, my love,' he murmured. 'In the nunnery, she will be in the care of the Goddess of Mercy—the God of War, who must be our companion, would frighten her to death with his red face and popping eyes!'

Ko-chin froze and he answered at once the question her lips could not frame: 'Ever since that little one was born I have had nightmares about how you would be treated with only a daughter, and what horrors would lie ahead for her. So, if you will come with me, wife, we will take our chance together in Japan.'

If she would come! They crept into the room where their daughter lay sleeping and Han-lao whispered, 'I have already found a bodyguard for you both! A young man whose last job was to wait outside the law courts until some rich offender engaged him as whipping boy. I was appalled by all those undeserved scars on his back, but he sees it all quite logically: he had committed no crime himself, so it was no loss of face for him to be beaten—an honest livelihood in its way but he feels it could be improved upon! So . . . '

'Your first soldier of fortune comes with us,' smiled Ko-chin, lifting the baby into her arms. 'And here is mine!' So much mysterious potential in so small a frame . . . what would this child become? Ko-chin thought then of another girl, one who had never had a moment's real chance. 'My husband,' she murmured, 'as yet our daughter has no name. Perhaps, in memory of the Emperor's lost Pearl Concubine . . . ?'

'Pearl is the perfect name for her,' he answered softly. 'Remember how I told you once of the great stone dragons in the Forbidden City, straining to grasp the Pearl of All Knowledge and All Power? Well, one day, this little one will find new knowledge and powers beyond her parents' wildest dreams!'

At last the time had come to be glad when a girl was born, thought Ko-chin, still hardly able to believe her fortune. She knew already that there would be fear and war and constant struggle in the years ahead; change was never easy, but it was far, far better than to live condemned, at 17 years old, to the backwater of history. Thanks to this daughter of hers, she would be part of the great revolution brewing abroad!

Together, she and her baby turned to Han-lao's enfolding arms. 'May Kuan-yin, Goddess of Mercy, keep us all,' she whispered. 'She who saves the faithful from peril.'

But in the Forbidden City . . .

               . . . no Goddess of Mercy looked down with compassionate eyes upon the imprisoned Emperor. The one person that mattered to him was gone, her moonshine radiance drowned in deep water. In the midst of splendour, he decayed. Despised, and utterly excluded, he spent his days drawing paper dragons. Then on their backs he wrote the name of the man who had betrayed him to his aunt and, shredding them, sent them fluttering through the air.

Sometimes he remembered how, when he was a child, his tutor had brought him first toys, then books, from the Western world; and he would giggle to himself, recalling the day he had so nearly come to grief on the two-wheeled contraption called a bicycle.

On other days, though, he only remembered how he had brought his country to grief: condemned by the foreign nations for 'crimes unprecedented in human history, crimes against the law of nations, against the laws of humanity and against civilization', somehow now the government must find £67 million: the blood money set for 66 dead at the Legations, 247 martyred missionaries, 30,000 butchered Chinese converts. In the Penitential Decree his aunt had forced him to issue he had shouldered the blame for all those crimes himself—but he had never wanted to fight the foreigners! He had wanted to learn from them. What had been so wrong in that?

Things should have been so different. What fun he and the Pearl had once had with the foreign gadgets, especially when they had startled dignified guests invited to sit upon the velvet chair with a music box concealed beneath . . . The Emperor sighed and said wistfully to the indifferent eunuch guarding him, 'Her Majesty has so many pictures of herself, and even of you eunuchs, taken by those Western cameras. We wish we might try it, too . . . ' Then he went back to his drawing of impotent paper dragons that would never seize for him the Pearl of All Knowledge and All Power.

When at last the poison came, he barely wondered who had sent it. His aunt, so near her own end now? He did not think so. His lips curled back: far more likely the man who had betrayed him to her, lest he come to power again. But it did not matter now . . . in agony with stomach cramps, his life burned away in apartments where the dust lay deep and no eunuch came near to care for him.

When, in far away Japan, Ko-chin heard of the death of the Kuang-hsu Emperor, 'of Glorious Succession', she did not grieve, for now the spirit of the Pearl Concubine would be lonely no longer. And beside her a new Pearl, with a very different destiny, chuckled, and wriggled toes that would never be broken.

'WHEN A GIRL IS BORN'

On 14 November 1908 the Kuang-hsu Emperor died. The next day his aunt died. The new Emperor, a three-year-old child, was to be the last of a line which had ruled for over 250 years . . .

THE MANCHU DYNASTY

In 1644 Manchurian forces had swept down from the north into China to set an emperor of their own on Peking's Dragon Throne.

In 1793 the Manchu Emperor, pinnacle of a magnificent empire respected worldwide, was approached by the British: this fledgling western empire wished to trade with the ancient Celestial Empire, whose troops had marched further from their capital than ever Roman soldiers had marched from Rome. The Emperor refused. China was not interested in extending trade with 'barbarian merchants', nor did she wish to learn of the barbarian religion. Loftily he dismissed the British with: 'My capital is the hub and centre about which all quarters of the globe revolve . . . Tremblingly obey!' And that, as far as he was concerned, was that.

The British, though, quite apart from the snub to their pride, had no intention of letting a potential market of 400 million customers slip through their fingers—especially not when they had a glut of Indian-grown opium to sell for silver.

In 1839 in an attempt to stop the opium trade, China's antiquated warships fought British steam vessels which were equipped with modern arms. Their humiliating failure forced the Chinese into giving the British more trading rights—and ceding Hong Kong to them. Across the world, greedy eyes gleefully noted this first crack in the façade of imperial might and demanded *their* share of the 'Chinese melon'. As the Chinese economy staggered under the ensuing flood of foreign imports, rebellion flared against the Dynasty—and was only crushed with the help of the foreign powers raping the country. The carve-up of China's Celestial Empire went on apace.

In 1860 when the Chinese tried to shake free, British and French troops occupied their capital city.

In 1894 the despised Japanese, who had been modernizing since 1870, took chunks of Chinese territory for their own. Panic stricken, the Kuang-hsu Emperor himself rushed through Western-style reforms too little and too late. In a land racked by poverty and famine, the people erupted in the frenzy of despair and outrage which was the Boxer rebellion.

In 1900 the bloodsoaked streets of Peking were an augury of the huge bloodletting to come, as China, contemptuously dubbed by the world as the 'sick man of Asia', staggered into the twentieth century.

THE CHINESE REPUBLIC

In 1911 the last Manchu Emperor of the last dynasty was toppled. For young Chinese, sent abroad to study and seeing their country as others saw it, the blame lay not with the West but with their alien Manchu rulers. In Japan, where revolutionary Chinese could find safe haven, Sun Yat-sen co-ordinated worldwide Chinese student groups with the underground movement in China to replace imperial rule by a Western-style republic. But, that achieved, foreign gunboats still patrolled Chinese rivers, and the stranglehold of age-old customs still choked all real progress.

In 1915   Sun was ousted by the general who had betrayed the Kuang-hsu Emperor to his aunt, who now declared himself emperor. Japan was making huge new demands on Chinese territory. By the time the general died, provincial warlords rampaged, and government was a shambles.

In 1919   on 4 May, there were huge student demonstrations against the cowardice of China's leaders in the face of Japanese demands. This was the day when the true struggle against foreign domination, and for national regeneration, began. The success of the Russian Revolution, which had seized power by a mass movement, fired young Chinese intellectuals: from their universities they went to factories and villages to preach revolution to their own people.

In 1921   with Russian help, the Chinese Communist Party was founded, and Sun's revived Nationalist party armed. Young men were sent to Russia for military training. In the cities, unions, demonstrations, and strikes were organized by the Communist Party against the appalling working conditions of China's new industries.

In 1925   Sun Yat-sen died. One of the Russian–educated young men, Chiang Kai-shek, became the Nationalists' new leader and soon revolution was no longer on the agenda. The warlords, the wealthy, and the landowners were Chiang's allies, and they wanted the young Communist Party's activities stopped.

In 1927   Chiang, helped by foreign forces, launched his White Terror to exterminate the Communist 'bandits'. They fled to the mountains, there to begin creating a Communist Party whose propelling force would be, not, as in Russia, the urban working classes, but the peasantry.

From 1927 to 1949 war was continuous:

In 1931   the Japanese invaded China. It took fourteen years to expel them; then there were four years more of carnage as Communists fought Nationalists for the right to rule.

In 1949 the Nationalists, defeated, fled to Taiwan. The prediction of a young revolutionary Communist leader, Mao Zedong, had proved correct: 'several hundred million peasants will rise like a mighty storm. . . so swift and violent that no power, however great, will be able to hold it back.' The Chinese Communists had won the people's hearts by breaking the stranglehold of the past: landlords had been smashed, the peasants given their own land; women had new rights (and footbinding been declared a criminal offence); education was for all; and above all, the people had been given their own army. During the long years of war its soldiers moved among the people they served 'like fish in water'; no enemy could pin them down, nor predict where they would strike next.

In 1949 in Tiananmen Square in Peking—now known as Beijing—Mao Zedong proclaimed the 'People's Republic of China'.

But the huge revolution in a China still caught between past and future, between her own traditions and new ideas from the West, has not ended. Millions more died under the rule of Mao Zedong, 'Emperor of Communism'. And, just as on 4 May 1919, on **4 June 1989** young people crowded Beijing's Tiananmen Square, protesting against the government of Mao's aged successor and demanding 'democracy'. When they refused to disperse, units of the People's Liberation Army, the fruit of so many dreams, massacred an unknown number of those it had been created to serve.